A Meal f
Man in Tails

and other stories

Scottish Arts Trust Story Awards
Volume Three

Edited by
Sara Cameron McBean
and Michael Hamish Glen

Scottish Arts Trust

 Scottish Arts Trust
Scottish Charity number SC044753

Cover: *White Wedding* by Gordon Mitchell

ISBN: 9798481566450

Scottish Arts Trust
Registered Office:
24 Rutland Square Edinburgh
EH1 2BW
United Kingdom

Other publications from the Scottish Arts Trust

The Desperation Game and other stories from the Scottish Arts Trust Story Awards 2014-2018 (Volume 1) Edited by Sara Cameron McBean and Hilary Munro (2019)

Life on the Margins and other stories from the Scottish Arts Trust Story Awards 2019-2020 (Volume 2) Edited by Sara Cameron McBean and Michael Hamish Glen (2020)

Rosalka: The Silkie Woman and other stories, plays and poems by Isobel Lodge (2018)

Contents

The Armadillo
by Sarah Burke

Winner, Scottish Arts Club Short Story Competition 2021

He sat on the hallway stool to do up his shoes, as he did every morning. He fumbled with the laces. His fingers were stiff and his knuckles were swollen. He paused, bracing himself as he pushed his weight downwards through his hands onto his knees to stand up. He took his jacket from its peg and put it on, grappling with the zipper until the ends went together and then pulling it purposefully up.

He opened the door and stepped outside, as he did every morning. He closed the front door behind him, turned the key and gave the door a push to check it was secure. He turned to look out across the street. The last few days had been damp – a grey drizzle had hung around. It was a little brighter this morning. The air was still. It was the sort of weather that was in limbo, as if waiting to decide what to do. There were some darker clouds gathered in the west.

"It could go either way," he thought.

He would walk down to the high street to buy his newspaper, as he did every morning. The bin lorry rumbled at the bottom of the road. A seagull landed on a neighbour's roof, shocking the morning with its coarse cry. He gave it a disapproving look. Then, as he set off to go down the road, something caught his attention.

John McNair's life was all about routine. It had to be. He would wake every morning at seven o'clock. He no longer lingered in bed. He used to bring Cathy a cup of tea and they would sit in bed propped up on pillows, talking about all sorts of things before getting up. These days, he positioned a pillow sideways in the bed to fill the space she had physically left. And to avoid the other vacant spaces, he

1

went straight downstairs for his cup of tea and to get washed and dressed. He would go and get the paper. He would chat briefly to the shopkeeper and muster a cheery "see you tomorrow", despite the heavy sadness that it could be his only social contact that day. The walk home was harder than it used to be. He needed to pause to get his breath.

He made his porridge in the microwave and read the paper while he ate it, blowing on each mouthful. He could make the paper last until lunchtime. He read every word. The radio filled the silence. He microwaved a tin of soup for lunch and dipped his oatcakes in it. Cathy wasn't there to tell him not to slurp. He did the crossword in the afternoon. The afternoons were long. He might watch a film, listen to his audiobook, do chores, or write a letter. Cathy wasn't there reading or doing needlework in the green armchair. There was a Cathy-sized concaved imprint on that chair. The cushions had moulded around her shape. She wasn't in the garden tapping on the window asking him for a cup of tea. He had stopped going to the golf club. He no longer knew what to say to people.

A while back, people would still bring round a meal or ask him over for dinner. That had stopped. He'd never been good at social arrangements. A microwave dinner; the news; a shower. Then a whisky to get to sleep quickly so as not to miss the warmth, the smell, the rhythmic, quiet snoring of Cathy. Routine and repetition were like a comforting heartbeat, helping him to pass the time.

This particular morning, his attention was caught by a small, rounded, dark thing in the road. He put his hands on his knees and bent down to get a closer look. What was it?

Then Archie Henderson from number 15 stepped out of his front door. He had started his morning by making his wife, Linda, a cup of tea and helping her out of bed. He made her breakfast and counted out her tablets. She would be feeling better once they kicked in. They would be looking

2

after their grandson today. Their daughter would be dropping him off soon. It was exhausting (neither of them liked to admit this) but they loved every minute. Little Callum brought laughter and tears. Archie would nip down to the shops to get things for lunch – toddler food – white bread, cheese and ham to be cut into small squares, some grapes. And some sweeties, as a treat, and for cajoling him when needed. He could be a wee tyke.

"Morning John!" he called. John was bent over something in the road. He looked up and nodded.

"Archie!" he said in acknowledgement.

Archie was poised to get in the car, but instead strode over to John. "What have you got there?" he asked. The two men looked at each other.

John shrugged, "I've no idea!".

Archie also put his hands on his knees and bent over. The two men stood like this for a few moments, alternatively shaking their heads and frowning.

"What is it?" asked Archie.

John shrugged again.

"Is it alive?"

"I can't tell."

They both stood up and sank their hands into their pockets. John had his head on one side. Archie rocked back and forth from heel to toe. He had been a headmaster. It was his authoritative, thinking stance.

The sound of a door opening and shutting made them both look up. Jenny from number 9 was stepping out of her house. Her small dog bounded at her feet.

"Morning!" she called breezily, smiling and striding past them – her youthful energy in stark contrast to their own. She often took the dog for a walk in the morning, after her children spilt out of her front door at 8:30am in a noisy kerfuffle. There were four of them, often squabbling or pulling at each other – sending energy and noise up and down their street in eddies and whirlpools of turbulence. Jenny would often be out for an hour or so. John would see her leave as he left for his paper. She would get back as he was washing up his porridge bowl.

"I think it might be a wee creature," said John.

"Aye," said Archie, "but what is it? I've never seen anything quite like it."

"I'm not sure. It's like a…I don't know. It looks like it's sleeping."

"It's a funny place to sleep!"

"You don't suppose it's dead?"

"Maybe…but it just looks curled up."

A car turned into the end of the road. Archie and John looked at each other alarmed – Archie quickly outstretched his arms and stepped to one side, guarding the 'thing'. The car slowed and gave the pair a wide berth as John waved the car on.

John blew air into his cheeks. Archie raised his eyebrows in relief.

"Well, we can't leave it here," said Archie.

"Will we give it a wee poke and see what it does?"

"We will need to get a stick – it could be vicious."

"I could go and get a stick, I suppose."

They stood for a few moments longer.

Archie went closer and went to nudge it with his boot.

"Dinnae kick it, Archie," John intervened, "it's just a wee thing, you'll frighten it…it might retaliate."

"I was just going to give it a wee nudge."

"A wee nudge with that boot of yours! It might bite if you scare it!"

"Oh, well, you're probably right."

"Let's just watch it a while longer. It might be some kid's pet that's got away or a wee beastie from the woods."

They resumed their position, standing over it, hands in pockets.

4

"So how are things with you?" asked Archie awkwardly.

"The usual aches and pains. We're not getting any younger, are we?"

"No," he patted his rotund belly, "and I can't get rid of this."

"Could be worse though."

"Aye, that's true."

John nodded thoughtfully.

"I was thinking about you and Cathy the other day."

Cathy's name said aloud seemed to ricochet around John's whole being.

"Did you hear that there's a young couple moving into number 6?" continued Archie. "They're expecting a baby – just like you and Cathy when you moved in."

"Aye, and you had one already."

"Aye, Stuart will be 44 this year."

"What about those barbeques we used to have – at Dennis and Sheila's? Remember that one where their friend's kids came and were playing the fiddle and old Davey brought his guitar?"

"I remember! Dennis got out the whisky!"

They both chuckled.

"That was a good laugh!"

"A drunken fiasco! Remember Linda and Cathy dancing?"

"…the picnic table collapsed!"

"Oh aye!" They laughed. Then quiet again.

"That was 30 years ago."

"Thirty years, who would have thought!"

"We had some good get-togethers."

"We certainly did…thirty years!"

"Still here."

Silence settled.

"I'm sorry about Cathy," managed Archie.

John nodded. Again, the sound of her name sped around

his body, through his blood vessels, bouncing off the inside of his skin.

"We've not seen much of you since, you know…" Archie trailed off.

"It's OK," reassured John.

"Are you, you know, doing OK?"

"Aye," replied John, "I'm doing alright." And then, quietly, "I miss her."

His eyes were moist. He hadn't really spoken to anyone about her for months. It felt sad. It felt like relief. Archie put his hand on John's shoulder. John had an instinct to turn towards the touch, to be held, hugged. It had been so long. He looked steadfastly at the 'thing'.

Archie withdrew his hand and hesitated. "I'll get a stick," he said, but he didn't move.

"Is it some kind of reptile?" asked John, "It's looks leathery and scaly."

"Maybe. I was thinking it could be an armadillo."

"An armadillo!"

"Aye, I think so."

"An armadillo?" questioned John. "Are they not bigger?"

"Maybe it's a baby. It's got that kind of skin. I think armadillos curl up."

"What would an armadillo be doing here!" exclaimed John.

"Maybe it escaped from somewhere…I don't know!" They both chuckled.

"We could give the SSPCA a call – they could send someone out."

"That could take a while. We should probably try to move it ourselves".

John glanced at Archie and nodded.

"I'll go and get a box then," said Archie folding his arms above his belly and staying where he was.

"You two still here!" called Jenny coming behind them on

the same side of the road.

"Watch the dog!" cried John urgently.

"There's a wee creature!" expanded Archie, "we're trying to work out what it is!"

Jenny tightened her hold on her dog's leash and pulled it back. She followed the men's gaze, then looked up at them. They were both sombre and earnest. She stepped closer to the 'thing'.

"Careful now!" interjected John.

Jenny kicked the 'thing' briskly with her foot – John and Archie gasped in horror.

She scooped it up in her hand and grinned at John and Archie. She turned it over and showed them the underside – it was hollow. They stared in disbelief and confusion.

"It's half an avocado skin," she announced. Avocado flesh had been scraped out of the gnarly, dark casing. "I will stick it in my compost bin!" she called behind her as she strode towards her house.

Archie and John stared after her, sheepishly looked at each other and then laughed, loud and long.

"Well I never."

"Who would have thought!"

"Perhaps you'd like to come around for some dinner sometime later in the week?" said Archie.

"Aye, I'd like that," replied John.

"I'll get a date with Linda then," he smiled and gave John a pat on the back. "It looks like it's going to be a nice day...there's blue sky up there!" he said, gesturing above the roofline.

He crossed the road and got in his car. John watched him start the engine and drive off up the road. He turned to walk down the hill. He was late getting his paper.

Quantum Postcards
by Laura Quigley

Second Prize, Scottish Arts Club Short Story Competition 2021

She's washing an elephant in Stanley Park when two old ladies appear by the lake. "Edith Sharma, in't it?" "Aye, that's Edith." She turns, silenced, but it's enough for them to know they're right. Like time's gone back sixty years to the Copacabana Coffee Bar, where they tutted, rolled their eyes and muttered, "Mrs Paki."

Love from Gwen and Carol. Blackpool.

At university, young Edith's reading physics, defiant of her mother's expectations, but out in the damp air, smoking by the cathedral wall, she feels lost. That's when she first sees him. He's not lost but he's looking for something more than the beatnik crowd around him, and his brown eyes linger, curious to see a woman so alone. A gold signet ring gives him a regal air she'll discover isn't justified. She stamps out her cigarette and follows him inside.

Love from Siddharth Sharma. Not from Pakistan.

Their first touch, quietly desperate, in her small, shared room. His kiss tastes of beer and ginger and she trembles, and they laugh that they're both new at this, but his moonlit caress is kind. The bright morning though is awkward. She studies his movements but can't figure why she feels so out of phase. She longs to see herself as he sees her, but she's first to look away as he departs for class. When Edith surfaces, her teasing room-mate declares she's picked out the perfect bridesmaid's dress already.

Love from Daphne. Room-mate. Out of touch.

Home's cold. Bringing him was a mistake, but he's so

eager, crackling with ideas. Blackpool's famous lights are strings of dead dripping bulbs and it's freezing on the piers, but that's still better than sitting among the disapproving whispers, and her mother looking through him as she fusses. They call him Sid because they can't pronounce his name. By the railings above the infinite beach, Edith listens to him, breathlessly alive while smothered in his coat, but also terrified and conscious of every stranger's eyes. She longs to run, but the tide's come in too fast to save her.

Love from North Pier, Blackpool, By the Sea.

First night they open, she feels she's drowning in Sid Sharma's Indian Palace Restaurant, built on a whim and not much money. Did she really go to university just for this? To wait on tables? Cash the till? Meet and greet like some witless air hostess her mother wanted her to be? A sandalwood Ganesh, the elephant-headed god who blessed their wedding, watches her relentless efforts to keep the place afloat. But Sid's cooking up a storm to serve their customers any dish they want – English, Indian, French, Moroccan. Have fragrant pilau rice with your steak and kidney pie. The menus always changing, the clientele are paying and it all feels so exotic with skiffle on the sitar and the papadums piled high.

Love from Sharma's Palace. Please Come Again.

One morning's headlines force Sid to take stock. He slows down to read the papers. They're exhausted, too busy for more than the occasional brush against each other as they wipe the bar or argue in front of kitchen staff. Her lips cannot recall the last time that he kissed her. He can't seem to bring himself to look her in the eye. She catches worrying phrases and a photo of a burnt-out shop, but it takes days for her to hear the whole story: three restaurants, all Indian, were invaded, smashed, incinerated. One she knows is painfully close to their old university. Now Unwelcomed. Hated. Conflagrated. There are frantic phone calls from his family in the middle of the night. Stop this nonsense Siddharth and come home.

Love from Rajasthan. Wish You Were Here.

Blackpool swells for the season. Every pier awash with singers, every pub vomiting visitors looking for a meal. Sid Sharma's firing up the business, despite the risk. Edith's intimidated by drunken revellers rowdy in the alley. They spit and she has to rush inside so no-one sees her crying. Sid cannot be allowed to see her crying. Frantic, she wipes their disgusting venom off her face. Morning brings "Go Home" and "Paki Bastards" daubed across their door. She seals up the letterbox to the restaurant, but threats still reach their little flat upstairs.

Love to Sid, you Paki-loving whore

In a sea of faces, Edith spots old schoolfriends, Gwen and Carol in their circle gowns outside the Winter Gardens. They're excited because they're seeing Tommy Steele from off the telly and they mock her when she doesn't know the man on all the posters. But of course "he's never sung in Paki-land". As a slow night closes, Sid's ready to shut the Palace when a knock brings in a customer eager for some quiet after a show. Edith sends Sid back into the kitchen for samosas, while she serves the late arrival their finest whisky at the bar. Ganesh smiles upon them, until at last there is goodbye and they laugh pleasantly when Sid says "good morning" not "goodnight". Edith turns to her husband in stunned delight: "That was Tommy Steele." As they collapse together into bed before the dawn, Sid murmurs his intentions – "Next time we shall ask him for a photograph."

Love from Tommy, with thanks to Sid and Edith.

Word gets round. Sid Sharma's Indian Palace becomes a late-night haven for entertainers looking for some peace. Awash with autographs on photographs, the bar's obscured by waves of smoking comics, fresh off the stage. The female singers prefer the booths and a tandoori with their personal security. Nights are long, but the days tranquil and with a little money coming, the Sharmas buy their first TV, amused to see all the famous faces sober.

Love from Shirley, Eric, Ernie, Tommy Cooper, Ken, Petula
and every band that ever played in Blackpool.

She wheels him through the zoo. Sid likes the elephants. Then onto Stanley Park, where they sit beside the lake. In the stillness, a tremor passes through them. He asks her name again. "Edith," she replies, patting his hand gently every time. His skin is sagging, his hair is white but so much is unremarkably the same. His crisp shirt beneath his fine-knit sweater. His polished shoes. Suspicious looks from a passing stranger. Sid's gaze lingers on her face, curious and, for the first time, Edith sees herself as he has seen her, an exquisite mystery in his eyes.

Love from your wife Edith, always by your side.

She serves him his memories, now he can't get out of bed. The photo album sits heavy on his legs, but his humour improves as he reads the autographs.

Love from Shirley. Love from Eric. Ernie. Tommy Cooper.

Each one a moment, his family photos. All that's left, but no regrets. They built everything together and with his leaving, the town they lived in seems to sink a little more each week into the sea.

Love from Petula. Love from Ken.

No more end of pier shows or singers. No more dances.

No more sea of circle gowns for Tommy Steele. No more Sid Sharma's Indian Palace Restaurant, now a gravestone she realises too late reminds her of the Specials menu.

Love from his wife Edith, forever in her heart.

Gwen and Carol remain, just two old ladies by the lakeside, peering at a memory who might once have been a friend.

"So what's with the elephant?" says Carol.

Gwen spots a sign: Fund-raising for Dementia.

Carol fetches a pound coin from her purse and Gwen drops it in the box.

They potter off.

Edith rolls her eyes and smashes the long-handled brush down into the bucket. Soap spills across the path. "Did they think I'd not remember?" she says through gritted teeth, but the elephant caresses tears and years away and she smiles at the creature in her care. The grey old boy's a rescue, scarred and battered by his caged days of entertaining. By the lake in Stanley Park, there was once an elephant-wash for the circus and now the zoo is giving it a go, all for charity of course. It's quite a turnout. Everyone loves the elephants. She'd never realised before today just how big they really are.

Love from award-winning Stanley Park, Nature's Heaven

Her charge leans his head a little lower and she sees herself reflected in the iris of his eye. But emerging from that dark matter, she can see another elephant and, in that elephant's eye, more darkness and another elephant, and another, like infinite Ganeshes, everlasting, the god himself sat beside her, laughing, sixty years before, as they listen to the tutting of silly women in the Copacabana Coffee Bar.

Love from Ganesh Chatuthi, Indian God.

Then it's her wedding day and Sid sits to have his feet bathed. He has exquisite, dancer's arches. In that moment she tells the Universe she loves this Siddharth Sharma and she knows how much she's loved. All else of this existence is just the scum she prays the sacred waters will simply wash away.

Love from the Happy Couple.

"Did they think I'd not remember?" She leans, breathless against the elephant's wrinkled hide, her heart beating that little bit too fast, but the Universe is recording this and every moment, like snapshots of her lifetime, postcards of her memories. She recalls the golden orbs of Siddharth's dying eyes, and knows at last the message he was reading as he died.

Love from the Universe. Across the Miles.

It's a beautiful day.

Inspired by a true story. Even the elephants.

A Meal for the Man in Tails
by Heather Parry

Third Prize, Scottish Arts Club Short Story Competition 2021

In Taoism, it's believed that a wake should last seven days and be held in the home. On the final night of the wake, the family of the deceased put out food for the deities that will escort the deceased's soul through the netherworld and into the beyond. The family often put out a delicate fish for the deity to eat, hoping that the difficulty of picking the meat from the bones will give them more time with the departing soul of their loved one.

MENU
amuse-bouche
braised kohlrabi with roasted garlic and truffle oil

The table is set for one. She places the cold dish on top of the slate and adjusts the cutlery beside it. It has been a long time since she's laid the settings herself. In the kitchen, behind her, things sizzle and steam, different courses prepped and pre-cooked and ready to come together. She tries not to think of the tiny box in the next room, the box that has been there for seven days now. She wipes her hands on her unwashed chef's jacket and tries to quiet her trembling. Last time the man had come, she had not been expecting him. This time, she is prepared.

He does not knock. He pushes open the door and sweeps in, the tails of his dress coat swimming in his stead. His waistcoat is expensively tailored. His trousers have the perfect crease. His tie is tastefully colourless, twisted and turned into a half Windsor, and above it there is a face with no eyes, just a mouth and a nose. The man gently closes the door and takes his seat at the table, brushing his tails out from under him.

As if called, a baby girl crawls in from the next room. She is painted in watercolours, the carpet faintly visible beneath her, just as her father was when he emerged from his box to meet his chauffeur. The baby girl seats herself in the middle of the dining room floor to wait.

salad:
marinated beetroot with goat's cheese

She takes a crisp white, fruity not tart, from the fridge and twists out the cork. She flinches as her bicep brushes against her swollen breast, the inflamed tissue sensitive through her shirt. She carefully fills his wine glass as he delicately slices what's in front of him. The constituent parts of the dish are spread as far away from each other as they can be, so he has to slice the beetroot and get it on his fork, then slice the cheese and get it on the fork, to eat each nuanced mouthful. With good manners, each bite takes just that little bit too long. She smiles. She must play the game for a while longer, must make him comfortable, must make him briefly forget his charge. She keeps herself from looking at her child, on the floor, sitting upright. Baby girl always had a strong back.

Hospitality; pure hospitality and nothing more. She is Michelin-starred and she is merely extending a professional hand to her guest, a person that comes by as part of his work. The child on the floor between them is incidental. When the meal is over, the man will take her baby, her watercolour baby, away from the living world and onto the place she will reside. The meal is simply a courtesy. That is what she wants him to believe.

She lets him sit for a few minutes when he has finished. His vague odour of wet soil and rot intrudes as she takes the neatly emptied plate in front of him.

appetiser:
steamed asparagus with caramelised red onions,
Hollandaise and boiled egg

He nods as she presents the dish, a small tilt of the head to acknowledge the artistry of the arrangement. The egg sliced impossibly thin, the onions neither soupy nor browned, the asparagus beneath it all, fresh green and bright as day.

He eats so smartly, so slowly, his movements considered. She has seen it before, in the manner of the funeral directors that dealt with her husband. Unobtrusive, inoffensive, mindful of the fact that though your presence may be necessary, nobody wants you there. She recalls that tomorrow those same men will return for her daughter's body. She puts the thought far from her mind.

She looks over his shoulder at the girl. The baby seems to have grown since her death, seems to have filled out in the cheeks and in her creased thighs, though it may just be that the outlines of her are less distinct than they were before.

seafood:
flash-fried octopus with fennel and orange

The plate is overloaded. The octopus is overcooked. It took all her effort to watch it fry in the pan for two, three, four minutes longer than she should have allowed, but it pays off when she watches his jaw struggling with the rubbery flesh, masticating it into something more edible, giving her more time, more precious time.

As he chews, she steps backwards, just out of his sight, and turns towards the shape of the child. Her body aches to feed the baby. She lowers herself and extends her hand, though she knows that there is nothing to touch. Nothing physical. Last time the man with no eyes came, she reached out to touch her husband and her palm slid right through him. But she reaches out regardless and again finds nothing there that is real.

fish:
beer-battered mackerel with English mustard, cucumber and
radish

It took her half an hour to choose the fish, bringing each candidate close to her face and squeezing its midsection between her fingers. As she paid, the man behind the counter admonished her for excessively handling the produce. She will not be able to go to that fishmonger again.

On the plate, the mackerel is piled in chunks next to the crisp vegetables. The presentation is awful, truly horrendous and the fish was not suitable for the deep-frying process, but now each crispy parcel contains the danger of pain. The batter will stop the man from sliding the meat cleanly from the many small bones. He will have to pluck tenderly through every piece, or sit picking the sharp fragments from his mouth after each bite. She doesn't care which.

She no longer stands on ceremony as he begins to pick through the inconvenient dish. She crouches on the floor next to her child. She reaches out and stops herself. Instead, she says the girl's name: *Emmy. Emmy, please.*

She does not say come to me, let me hold you, let me protect you from where this man is going to take you. She merely opens her arms wide: Come to mummy.

The child looks up at her mother. She smiles. She does not move.

The woman reaches across her chest and unbuttons the jacket from the top. She pulls the jacket open and reveals a bra that is soaked at both nipples. She peels the triangle of material from one cup and gasps as she rips the wet breast pad from her skin, tearing dry milk with it. She holds herself in one hand and looks at the baby's mouth. She says *Emmy, Emmy come.*

The girl feels her mother's need and starts to crawl. Her mother coaxes her closer, closer, wiping milk from her nipple and saying the baby's name. The baby shuffles towards her mother, her mouth hanging open, her impulses still having some effect, but she stops. She looks at her mother, looks at her breast, mottled red and puffy, then tilts her head.

Emmy, Emmy please.

The baby turns around and crawls away from her mother, towards the table, closer to the man she belongs to now.

Her mother buttons the jacket up again, wraps both forearms across her chest and squeezes herself until the pain is almost too much to bear.

entrée:
roast duck with cherries and ginger

She doesn't bother slicing the bird, serving it whole, with a handful of the gingered fruits thrown on the side. The plate clatters from her hands as she serves. Jus tips onto the placemat and she dabs at it with a napkin. She mumbles a sorry but doesn't notice when he raises his hand to refuse the apology, as she is already on her knees, crawling towards the baby girl.

She grabs at the figure. She holds onto nothing. She says the girl's name over and over again: *Emmy, Emmy, Emmy.* The girl sits behind the man, watching his back, not taking her eyes off the man and her mother can do nothing but plead.

He takes forever to eat the dish and the whole time, she tries.

18

remove:
chestnut and wild mushroom risotto with Taleggio

She plops a ladleful of the rubbery rice into a bowl; it slops over the sides. She tosses it in front of him and he makes no attempt to excuse her serving style.

He is struggling now and leaving longer between bites. The dish is claggy and each forkful sticks to the roof of his mouth, making his tongue work to free the food and let him swallow. It is no good to her. The child is looking up at her chaperone, her new protector. The child is ready to go. The woman weeps.

sweet:
summer berry and mascarpone tart

The tart, of course, is too easy to consume. If she could make it again, she'd have filled it with glass.

dessert:
pears poached in sloe gin with vanilla

She sits opposite him and pushes the bowl across to his place; it slides awkwardly, spilling the crimson gin reduction all over the white cloth. She slams the liquor bottle onto the table and reaches over to take his wine glass from where it sits. She gulps down the remaining Borolo and pours the burgundy spirit almost to the rim.

She is breathing hard and staring his way. He slices so fucking calmly, dips the fruit on his fork into its liquid, lifts the morsel to the end of his face. His lips peel back from his teeth and he sets the sweet pear onto his tongue. She wishes she had bolted the door instead of setting the table.

after dinner:
coffee and a truffle

She slams the slate platter down in front of him, breaking off a corner and tipping over the chocolate cubes, but cannot let go of the edges of it. Her fists won't ungrip. She starts to keen, not quietly, but hysterically, with abandon. He pushes his chair away from the table and lets her fall into his lap, her legs touching and to the side, a child herself now. He holds her, never moving his head, barely touching, a mother for a moment. She stops heaving, stops making those sounds, but makes no attempt to move. He reaches past her to take a truffle with his fingertips and, very slowly, politely, sticks out his tongue and places the truffle on it. There are three truffles on the platter. When the three are gone, she knows she has to get up.

He swallows the third. She gets up.

to finish:
a goodbye, no tip

He finishes his meal and dabs his napkin at the corners of his mouth. There is no bill to pay, no debt to settle, so he stands up slowly and puts his hand to his stomach, turning towards the woman and bending slightly at the waist. The woman makes no response. She has little to say.

The watercolour girl at the floor watches the man with no eyes, willing him to come to her, opening her arms up to his embrace. He leans down towards the child and lifts her upwards, tucking her small body into the crook of his arm. As they leave, the man turns, as if to glance once more at the mother behind him, but there are no eyes, there is no baby, there is no one to see.

The Oak Woods
by Louise Farquhar

Winner, Edinburgh Award for Flash Fiction 2021

There are questions to ask, answers to find. Hand in hand we walk and walk through the Salen oak woods, past ancient trunks gnarled with moss and bark. The earth, thick with amber leaves, falls steeply to the river's bank where branches ride the tangled water until caught by pewter rocks. Children call to each other through the faint whisper of the trees, their bright jackets darting like fireflies in the dusky light. They bring our walk to life. I think of the time passed since the first test, when we waited for the colour change, surprised when it didn't. Was it me? Was it him? Time and tests came and went, like the ebb and flow of the river, until facts showed it to be us both. It was pleasing to know; our loss became blameless.

Tendrils push upwards at our feet, the saplings of these woods birthing for long days ahead of knots and lichen and old age. I dreamt of birds last night, layered in rows, finely balanced on narrow branches, orderly and expectant. I think of them now, as a hooded crow sweeps overhead, choosing not to stop and gather like my ethereal friends. Our hands hold fast, thumbs and fingers weaved together. Yes, our answer is found, our questions eased, not to fade but to settle, just as the woodland quiets when night rests a dark head.

It was, and would be, just us.

Execution
by Kirsty Hammond

Second Prize, Edinburgh Award for Flash Fiction 2021

'Ayla McClymont, for your crimes of witchcraft, you are sentenced to death.'

Standing in the crowd, Catriona sees her friend crumble, desolation saturating every crevice of her face.

'It's not right,' whispers Margaret. 'She's no more a witch than I am. Is there anything we can do?' The executioner holds a flaming torch aloft as he trudges closer to Ayla. Her hands and feet are bound around a wooden stake and a pile of kindling reaches up, waiting to consume her. Her eyes dart over the crowd, unable to focus.

'Someone sacrificed Farmer Donald's sheep,' says Catriona, 'and Ayla's getting the blame. They won't change their minds now.'

'But she didn't do it!'

'Don't you think I know that?' The executioner reaches Ayla's side. 'It's too late. All we can do is watch.'

'I can't.' Margaret turns to leave. The voices around them surge and the women look back at the platform. The executioner is on his knees, his face reddening as he tries to take a breath that doesn't touch his lungs. Clawing at his neck, he looks out, begging, but he falls before anyone can reach him, blood dripping from his glassy eyes. The torch rolls harmlessly away.

As the crowd crushes forward, no one notices the bindings glide off Ayla's hands and feet, or see her waver for a moment before escaping. No one except Catriona, who pushes her spellbook, recently stained red, further into the folds of her coat and follows Ayla away from the crowd.

Three oh nine
by Laura Muetzelfeldt

Third prize, Edinburgh Award for Flash Fiction 2021

You can watch your feet like you're in a film, like it's not you walking. You just see the shoe go up, hit the ground.

She was out of breath, walking too fast. She looked at her watch. Three exactly.

"That you gonna get your Ryan a present, hen?" another mum asked.

A pause, a beat too long.

"Aye."

The shop was up by the school and the kids were streaming out and yelling. She wished she could've come another time. But it had to be now.

The door jingled as she entered.

"Ah, there you are. Thought you'd be wanting this," Mary said, holding up a football top just the right size for the age he was now.

The sight of it, bigger than the one from last year, made her fumble her purse. But Mary was already folding the top and gently sliding it into a bag: "Now you put that away."

Three oh six. She had to hurry.

Her eyes went down again, watching her feet go up, hit the ground. Up, hit the ground.

Then she stopped. She was here.

She looked at her watch, heart beating. Three oh eight. A minute early. She stood by the railing and waited.

The sound of a car getting nearer.

Three oh nine. The car passed, slowing down for the speed bumps that were put in.

She turned around, carefully took the top out of the bag and fixed it to the railing. Then there was quiet.

Vang Rooj
by Andrew Burnet

Winner, Isabel Lodge Award 2021
Shortlisted, Scottish Arts Club Short Story Competition 2021

Dawn came stealthily that morning, a cold grey light seeping through the curtains, and he knew it was almost time.

He lay on his side, wide awake but inactive, facing the dormant form of his wife, marvelling over the ribbons of pure white hair that snaked over her neck. Not a trace of the chestnut blaze of yesteryear, but still enough to feed his tender admiration.

The sensations of his own body began registering. One knee lying over the other, bones digging in. A gurgle of hunger in his belly. His eyes raw and watery from lack of sleep. In his loins, no feeling but a faint prickle of anxiety.

He reached up one hand and placed it on her hip, feeling the flesh through her nightie, withered but familiar and reassuring. On an impulse, he slid his hand forward, reaching for a fuller embrace, but his thumb snagged on a catch in the fabric. Instead, he laid his fingers over the curve of her thin ribs. He sighed.

A memory came to him then, one he'd not entertained for years. He and she were lying, much like now, side by side in bed. The room was small and smelt a bit odd, but the bed was cosy and accommodating. Sunlight poured in, convivial and bright, sliced into rays by the slatted wooden shutters. It was their honeymoon. They were in France.

From outside, he could hear voices from the nearby market: men and women exchanging greetings, making bargains, shouting warnings, laughing and gossiping. *Bavardage*, the French called it.

He picked up the delicious aroma of freshly baked

24

baguettes from the *boulangerie* and the exotic scent of coffee. His appetite stirred heartily, for it was late in the morning. The previous night, and every night since their wedding just six days ago, they had engaged in vigorous, joyful coupling, bashfully discovering each other, giggling as the bed groaned and creaked below them. Her flesh was generous and warm, plump and pliant. Low moans escaped between her parted berry-red lips. The smell of her overwhelmed him with desire.

He inhaled deeply through his nose, as though the inrush of air could summon back the scene from – when was it? – fifty-five, nearly sixty years ago. But his eyes opened, as he knew they must, to the time-served bedroom at home and a November morning scoured by a steely, low-lying sun.

At last, he lifted his side of the covers and levered himself from bed, feeling the ache in his old bones more intensely than ever. He made his way down the narrow stair, wincing a little, gripping the handrail for balance, and shuffled into the kitchen.

Propelled by habit, he crossed the room to the kettle and took it to the sink to fill, ignoring the silent reproach of the telephone in the corner. 'Time enough,' he murmured to the empty room, busying himself with tea and teapot, cup and saucer, spoon, milk and sugar. When the tea was ready, he sat in his usual seat at the bare table, gazing blankly through the window.

A lone bird was perched on a branch of the rowan tree, darting quizzical glances around the garden. Its plumage was black, save for a silvery hood around the neck and shoulders. A jackdaw, he decided vaguely.

Saint-Sauveur-le-Vicomte: that had been the name of the village. He congratulated himself for remembering that. A daunting medieval castle, a crumbling abbey and, not far away, a beautiful river. They had spent many happy hours strolling alongside that river, holding hands in the sunshine, stopping for a picnic, dipping their feet in the water.

25

One afternoon, in a café, they fell into halting conversation with an elderly local woman. From her they gleaned, in their classroom French, that there had been a terrible tragedy on this part of the river. A small boy had fallen in while larking around; a man had dived in to rescue him. Both had drowned, swept to oblivion by unseen currents. *'Prenez garde!'* she had admonished them with a friendly cackle. 'Be cay-fool.'

As they strolled back to their *pension*, she leant into him, made him stop, threw her arms around him and gazed into his startled eyes. 'Please don't ever die,' she said, in a thin voice that choked him with affection.

Later they managed to smile, even joke about it: this moment when darkness had been admitted to their tiny, private paradise. It became a thing they said to each other: 'Please don't ever die.' It was almost possible to believe in it.

But over time, they had stopped saying it. Grandparents departed; then parents. Friends suffered ghastly accidents or developed terrible diseases. Wars tore the world. Disasters shredded lives with terrifying indifference. And steadily, they grew older. Not dying was unachievable.

He finished his cup of tea and placed it empty in the centre of the saucer. Then he rose, pushing the chair back with his calves. He walked over to the telephone, picked it up and called the doctor's surgery.

To the young woman who answered, he said, 'Yes, good morning. I'd like to report that my wife died during the night … Yes, I'm afraid so. Yes.'

He gave some details. Name, address, date of birth. He had it all prepared. 'Seventy-eight … Yes … About 4am, I think. I was … No, not really, just … Yes, yes, I'll stay here. Thank you. Yes. Goodbye.'

He placed the phone back in its cradle and stood silently staring at it. He had been rehearsing the line for much of the night. Speaking it aloud had given his predicament

26

substance, in a way he hadn't foreseen. Fat hot tears bulged from his eyes. He felt them on his cheek, warm then cold. He raised a hand to his brow, shielding his grief, but there was no one to see it.

There were other calls he should make, but not now. Not yet. On wobbly legs, he struggled back up the stairs and returned to the bedroom. He sat on the bed and placed a comforting hand on her cold, dead arm. His throat tightened and his shoulders juddered. He hoped the tears would end before the doctor arrived.

On the last night of their honeymoon, he surprised her. He had put by just enough money for a slap-up meal, with a bottle of red wine. 'Vang rooj,' they called it, chuckling together. Proudly, he whisked his new wife to a corner bistro he had identified a few days earlier. '*Oui*,' he confirmed to the maître d'. '*Une réservation.*'

Their table was draped in white linen and they tittered behind the back of the pompous waiter with his moustache, black waistcoat and white apron.

'*Canard à l'orange?*' she giggled, incredulous and already a little tipsy.

'*Coq au vin!*' he replied, snorting with ribald laughter.

The waiter rose above the joke, tilting his chin up as he pencilled their order on his pad. But he read them well, looked kindly on them, ensured they were well fed.

When the bill was paid, he brought over two glasses of cognac. '*Aux frais de la maison*,' he told them with a brief smile. 'On ze 'ouse.'

It was the proper way to end a meal, when you were in France, on the last night of your honeymoon. They swirled the huge glasses, flushed and romantic, clinked them together, then forced down a fiery sip. He caught the anxious glint reappearing in her eye but, before she could speak, he placed a tender finger on her lips.

'I shan't,' he said. 'I promise. I shan't.'

Snap Chat
by Michael Callaghan

Winner of the Golden Hare Award 2021
Shortlisted for the Edinburgh Award for Flash Fiction 2021

I rush home as soon as the school bell goes and I'm there in 20 minutes. When I get in, Mum's on the sofa, watching *Pointless*. I ignore her and go to my bedroom. I'm keen to talk to Keira. We've been chatting for three days and we're getting along great. She's really cool and pretty. Unless her photo is well Photoshopped!

I log onto Kool-Krew. Keira's already logged on.

"Hi K. Wuu2?" I type.

A few seconds, then:

"Nowt much Olly. Bored."

"Not now, though? I'm here!"

"Typing's boring. LMRL."

I pause. *Let's meet in real life.* This was a development.

"For real?"

"Yeah. You told me you're near Edinburgh. Get the train to Waverley. I'll meet you outside Burger King at 6.30."

I smile.

"Hmmm. How well do I know you, Keira?"

"Ha! You don't. But how do I know you're really a 15-year-old schoolboy living with his mum?"

"True." I type. "Okay. I'll meet you."

"Cool. Don't be late."

I go downstairs. Mum looks up.

"You hungry son?"

"Nah. Going out."

Mum keeps staring at me.

"I worry about you, son. You spend all your time in that bedroom. Or you're out for hours and don't say where. You've had that dead-end school caretaker job for ten years.

You could … do so much better with your life."

I smile. "Don't worry, Mum."

I go to leave.

"Brian …" she calls. "Where're you going? Brian … *please* …"

I ignore her and set off to meet Keira.

The Reprisals
by Timothy Hemmings

Shortlisted, Scottish Arts Club Short Story Competition 2021
Editor's Choice, Scottish Arts Club Short Story Competition 2021

He looked up from the watch he was mending to see her waiting uncertainly on the threshold. Señor Roble rose to his feet as he had done all his life when a lady came into his shop, just as his father had taught him to, god rest his soul. He saw her hesitate, look down the street and then step inside out of the sun.

She took a watch from her handbag and asked him to appraise it. A Picot, Barcelona. It looked new. The second hands movement was strong and steady. He could see no fault with it. 'Señora, can you tell me what the problem is?'

'They are coming,' she said, looking at the watch, her eyes fixed on it as if she were assessing the need to buy a new strap. It was in perfect condition. With her eyes still on the timepiece she repeated 'they are coming, and they will shoot you. They will take you into the mountains, and they will shoot you.' She took the watch from him and flipped it over. ' Unless you hide the statue and hide it well.'

He gave her a look as if to say *What statue Señora?* But she had no time for pretence and dropped the timepiece into her bag and closed the clasp with a click. 'Sometime next week,' she said.

A passer-by might have assumed a simple conversation had taken place and she had decided against any work that the watch might have needed. Maybe the cost was prohibitive. There was a war on after all.

She wished him a good day and left. One of his legs buckled slightly as the door shut behind her. His palms were clammy with sweat.

Señor Roble had seen her many times before. She was a neighbour in the small fishing village of Sant Medir on the outskirts of Barcelona where the streets rose up the hill to an unassuming church of sun-bleached stone. Above the entrance, St Jordi endlessly ran a lance through a dragon. At the port, cats slept as they waited for the boats to bring in the catch. When they caught the whiff of fish they rose like snakes being charmed out of baskets to fight for scraps. Roble could hear them hissing at each other from his apartment.

In summer, a thin needle of light shone down streets so narrow two women laden with shopping could not pass, one of them would have to back up into a doorway to give the other right of way. This was usually decided by a mixture of status and age.

He couldn't remember the first time he had seen her. It would've been after the widowed sisters, Belen and Dolores, had moved out of the apartment across the street. His window looked directly into their place. Their washing lines faced each other. He had become accustomed to the widows' shawls hanging on the line, the shapeless black dresses and grey diaphanous bloomers that billowed and tugged in the breeze as if they were trying to escape – just as they must have grown used to his old vests and tired shirts.

By day, when the light was fierce, the sisters' amorphous figures had moved in the darkness of their apartment like deep sea monsters who came to the open window as if coming up for air. At night, he could see them hunched over their evening meal, listening to the radio.

One day they left, maybe to live with relatives in the city or into the country. The washing line was bare for a few weeks, and then it was suddenly full of children's clothes: shorts, tops, nappies, colourful dresses, a man's work clothes, so many pairs of tiny socks it looked like the line itself had come to life and was sprouting them. When he saw the new neighbour at the window he smiled, and she smiled back. At night when he glanced into their apartment, he saw the diorama of a young and happy family. He gave the children sweets whenever he happened to pass them in the street.

The war had come upon him slowly. At first it was something happening down south, in Madrid. Then he had heard arguments and fights in the bar at night. In the street, Lourdes, the blacksmith's wife, would not give way to Montse, the Mayor's wife because she was a 'Fascist.' In the end they both bustled past each other red faced and flustered.

One day, the washing line opposite had a uniform with a red, gold and purple flag, the flag of the Republic. Roble couldn't decide if he himself were a Fascist or a Republican. The air waves gave shrill accounts of revolutionaries and anti-clerical purges. The village priest disappeared, no one knew where. The church was locked up and quiet.

The statue was in the living room on a wall mounted plinth in clear of her apartment. Stella Maris, the Virgin Mary in a sky-blue cape, standing with her arms outstretched and her eyes full of compassion. She offered protection on the high seas and was the patron saint of the village. The statue had been in his family for generations. Señor Roble was fond of it even though it was thick with dust. She didn't look like an enemy of the Republic, but he took his neighbour's advice, wrapped the statue in a towel and hid it in the loft.

The night they came and beat on his door with the butts of their rifles, he put on his robe and let them in. In the posters around town the Republican forces were square jawed, muscular and heroic. They broke the chains of Fascism with their bare hands and shook defiant fists at German bombers. However, the soldiers at his door were young and skinny. Their uniforms sagged like an outfit on a ventriloquist's doll and they smelled of cheap wine, but their guns were real.

'We need to look around your place old man, for any counter revolutionary activity.' The tallest of the three spoke as if he were reading from a pamphlet. 'The enemies of the revolution are amongst us and must be dealt with for the Republic to flourish.'

They opened cupboards, looked in wardrobes and emptied out drawers onto the floor. Roble looked outside, the town was dark and quiet, though no one was sleeping. The tallest of the three, the leader, pointed to the empty plinth where the statue of the Virgin had been, her dusty outline was still visible on the wall.

'What was there?' The others stopped to look. Señor Roble stared at the space as well. His life depended on it.

'On the plinth?' Roble blinked and paused for a moment 'Ah, My trophy for excellence from the watchmakers' guild,' He embellished the lie a little more. '1932'.

The men with rifles considered this. If the virgin had been there in plain view, they could've smashed it and taken the old man down to the truck that waited at the docks but taking a man for the shape of something that wasn't there was harder to do.

'So where is it? This award?'

'The war effort. I gave it to the war effort.' Roble replied, his heart beating rapidly 'They needed metals to melt down for guns and ammunition.' He looked at their weapons as if he'd been personally responsible for their manufacture. It would be an irony of tragic proportions if he were to be shot with one of them.

They begrudgingly accepted his answer and left. He shut the door behind them, turned the lights off and lay on the bed and listened. In the darkness he could hear the muffled sounds of scuffles as the soldiers moved from apartment to apartment. By dawn, the truck was full and it took the prisoners away into the mountains. It was the end of a night that no one ever talked about.

Months later when the Republicans lost the war, Franco's Fascist forces swept into Barcelona and the reprisals began. Señor Roble never saw the neighbour's husband again, he could have died by firing squad or on the muddy banks of the Ebro where the fighting had been fiercest. There were so many black shawls now, around the shoulders of women too young to be widows or hanging from washing lines like flags of welcome for an army of vanquished ghosts.

He wanted to thank his neighbour for saving his life, but the air was charged with revenge, old scores were being settled and she was on the losing side of a rancorous Civil War. Food became scarce and there were no more sweets to offer her children.

He took a rickety old bus into the gothic quarter of Barcelona and walked the labyrinth of shiny cobbled streets until he found the one he was looking for: a row of antique shops with a fleet of model ships in their windows sailing in a sea of grandfather clocks, walking canes and snuff boxes. At the dealer's glass counter, he un-wrapped the statue with care; a stone gargoyle and a stuffed bear looked down at Stella Maris as the shop owner cast his eye over her.

He listened as the dealer reeled off his reasons as to why the statue was not worth what he might have supposed. However, he was going to stand firm on the price as it had been in his family for over a hundred years, and it had been costly when his grandfather had bought it. The edgings of her cape were covered with gold leaf.

On his way home, he reflected that the sum he had received would be enough to get her and her children safely over the border and into France and then further afield if necessary. In her apartment, he offered the envelope and she refused, but she did not protest when he put the money on the table and left.

A few days later her apartment was bare, the washing line limp. He thought about her and the children on the snowy paths through the Pyrenees and wished them well.

Wasps
by Marianne Taylor

Shortlisted for the Edinburgh Award for Flash Fiction 2021

Her thoughts were too slow and his too fast. His thoughts were his words, and his words were wasps, rushing in from all direction, each with a sting to deliver. They could not be evaded, endured or deterred. It was minutes or hours later when, exhausted, she decided to drop her arms and raise her head. She opened the front door and walked out into the street and they followed. Her head was in a cloud and the cloud was wasps. She measured her steps and counted her breaths in and out, to keep her slow thoughts ahead of her and away from the pain.

She followed the footways to the coast, stepped off the promenade and surfed down a steep shingle breaker to the shore. She undressed and, as she exposed more of her skin, so the wasps struck again and again. Her blood was slow and heavy with their venom. The stabbing stones softened under her feet as she walked into the water. The weight of the sea gathered and carried away her own weight. The stones fell away. The salt burned and soothed. The buzzing in her ears grew faint as the wild waves sang more loudly.

When she realised that the last wasp had fled back to land, she turned in the water to look at the frantic figure on the shore. But he was small now, distant, voiceless and harmless. She returned her gaze to the deep darkness before her and began to swim.

The Garden of England
by Chris Lee

Shortlisted, Scottish Arts Club Short Story Competition 2021

Follow the convoy. The biggest convoy in Europe. We spill off the M20 motorway in Kent and into a makeshift lorry park. There are thousands of us. This is like the great dock in Rotterdam, but without the organisation. My satnav is as good as anyone's but I've really got no idea where we are. Not that it doesn't happen all the time. When you're driving a long-haul truck, you can frequently end up in a named place, inside a bigger named place and you could point at a map and say, I'm in this city in this country, but when you look out of the window of the cab, well, it's just another grey, rain-swept holding pen. Today we're in England and time has stopped. Nothing is moving, nothing is happening, everything is in limbo. My life is quietly ticking and the world is quietly turning. And yet; it's absolute zero outside and nobody knows anything and there is no indication of when we'll be rolling. Oh, and I'm hungry and a bit dirty and well, good luck with getting any help with that.

We're a long way from my home town. You must have heard the joke. Where did Lech Walesa meet his wife? No? At a Gdańsk. That's where I'm from, Polish port on the Baltic. That's where my wife and kids are. They know I won't be home for Christmas. Never mind. I miss important dates all the time. That's what puts food on the table. My unreliability is reliable. The pay is good enough. But I don't make any promises. They live with it. I live with it. We've got WhatsApp in Poland too.

I am a connoisseur of rain patterns on the windscreen of a parked HGV. I see eternity, I see the history of the world. I patiently wait while Armageddon, the Big Bang and

Coronavirus all play themselves out, raindrop by raindrop. And sometimes I read and sometimes I watch a video. And sometimes, more often perhaps, I slump against the door. Not that I can't lie flat. This is a Volvo FH 2018. I'm in luxury. Just look behind me. That's a Russian plate, Kaliningrad. He's in a third-class travelling compartment compared to me. Practically cattle class. But that's what you get for not being in the EU. Oh sorry, sore point.

I shift my arse and realise I've been sitting on that book I've been meaning to start. Olga Tokarczuk, *Drive Your Plough Over the Bones of the Dead*. Olga is Polish and in Poland she is, well, she divides opinion. There are people who consider her to be a traitor who libels the Polish nation with her writings. For them she is an outcast and her books should be banned or burned, her awards taken back, her property seized. Their fury is that of medieval witch hunters. They claim that as Poland has been down for a long time and that now the country is rising to take up its true destiny, then the last thing it needs is one of its own being hypercritical. All true Poles must pull together. But what happens to untrue Poles? It's very hard to know sometimes where you stand in the eyes of the believers.

Then there are those who consider Olga to be a warrior for freedom. She has a Nobel prize, shouldn't we all take pride in that? And isn't what she says about the government true? Too much flag waving and denunciation. Shouldn't we all be past macho nationalism by now? But you really can't make up your mind until you've actually read something. So here it is, a book everyone tells me I have to read. And I will read it. Just not tonight.

You notice a lot of odd things out of the window as you're driving across the world. Not so much when you're motionless, but right now there are two people walking towards this truck. A man and a woman. And they are carrying something. And they look Indian. And the man is wearing a blue turban. They are both immaculate. They are smiling at me; they are offering me something. And there are more of them approaching the other trucks. A whole delegation of Indian people, British Indians, Sikhs in fact, as they tell me themselves, bearing food. They have come to feed us. That's extraordinary.

Inevitably, it is delicious. Not what I'm used to, but delicious nonetheless. Of course, I often dream about pierogi, golabki, sernik and makowiec as I hurtle along the motorways, autoroutes and autobahns of my domain. But you can't always get Polish food. And I'm not fussy and I've no idea why a bunch of anonymous truckers has been fed by a Sikh community, here in the Garden of England. But I tell you what, I am nourished and grateful and utterly dumbfounded.

What to do on a full stomach but slumber, quietly, in the warmth of the cab? It's my home after all. I spend so much of my life here. Does the trucker love his truck? Of course, he does. Take pride, take joy, in keeping your cab clean. You never know who might pop by. And sure enough, as darkness falls, out of the shadows, curiosity creeps. Perhaps 'yearning' might be a better way to describe him. He has found us out, he knew we would be here. But what is he? Who is he? A thin English youth, I can't see more from this distance, but I can sense him moving towards me. I don't know fully how this happens. There is a certain magic to it. Mind you, with a lorry park of thousands of vehicles and drivers from every corner of the globe, he is bound to strike lucky. That is, if he's careful not to be struck himself by hatred or fear. We truckers are not, I would say, a tolerant lot, if you take us as a whole. But he is very careful and very selective and I might not even satisfy his need, even if I am acknowledged as belonging to the world of his quest. And he is everywhere, believe me; in every town, in every place where our desire congregates. He comes close, he questions and I open the door.

Fifteen minutes later and we are done. He has slunk off into the night and I am a married man with a family again. It was a momentary excursion into another universe, it was a temporary feeding of the ache. It was, oh it was whatever excuse I find on the day. It was good, it was simple, it was sex.

Now I do need to sleep, there aren't going to be any facilities in this makeshift concrete wasteland, so I'll relieve myself quickly under the trailer and hop back into the warmth. But my dreams are restless. They always are, I've got Europe in my head. Roads, roads, roads. Bridges, flyovers, slipways and service stations. I feel the endless motion in my blood, I am hurtling into the wet rainy night and the streetlights are flashing like neurons. I drag the horizon towards me, klick after klick. I drive into sunrise. I drive across vast empty plains and up switchback mountain tarmac. I crawl in the crawler lane, I put the hammer down on the straight. I am speeding toward the vanishing point of life and then I burst out into a new day, hauling containers to infinity. I am pure diaspora. I surge in with the tide and I ebb away without a trace. I bring Poles to Newcastle. I see Geordies in Warsaw. The rivers are running with people. Africans in Dortmund, Chinese in Dublin, Mexicans in Naples, Filipinos in Reims. Listen; on the warm summer breeze, on the biting winter wind, you can hear, carried in the air, the unmistakeable sound made by the irresistible flow of people. Humanity on the march. You think you can stop that King Canute? Europe cast out its net centuries ago and now it teems with what has been caught.

I am a trucker. Most British people I meet think I'm a plumber. All Poles are in the building trade. Go back to where you came from, but fix my toilet first. Occasionally I'm an entrant for World's Strongest Man, but never sadly, a pianist or a physicist. What about Chopin? What about

Marie Sklodowska Curie?

I'm fogged up and bleary. And I come to in the slack grey light of an English morning. Where am I? Oh yes, going nowhere. I find my phone and call home. It's not too early, they're ahead of me in Gdańsk after all. And as soon as I hear a voice, a flood of guilt and sorrow and regret, and shame and resentment and bloody-minded defiance, and something close to love, crashes over me. I urge comfort and protection across the satellite highway, into the kind warmth of our apartment. I speak to my wife and feel her doubts and forgiveness, and something else. The ever so gradual pulling away from needing me. Did she ever need me? I'm a soul in permanent transit. I check in only to check out. I notice my children growing, but always in spurts. I have a jump cut edit of their lives because the spaces in between I just don't see. Each time we are together they are different people; they have outgrown my last memory of them. I tell myself we are allies in absence. But I've chosen this life, I'm shackled with it. They are fed and clothed by my long-distance calling. And then we come to a close. Goodnight, miss you, talk to you soon. Stay safe. Whatever that means.

Low rumblings send vibrations through the ground. We have a herd mentality in the HGV club. Ignitions fire up all around. This could be a false alarm of course, but it could equally be the signal for actual movement. And as we have no idea what the plan is, we'll take a half kilometre advance over stasis any day. We roll our great army of trucks out onto the road. We get ready to edge by slow, and even slower degrees. There's a fifty centimetres per hour speed limit in force. If this goes on much longer, we'll have killed all life in Kent with our emissions.

But as ever, the glacial progress at least enables me to look. And this morning, as the murky water vapour thins and is dispersed by the feeble rising sun, the port of Dover

41

looms into view. We are heading down to the great jaw of the dock, an endless line of trucks, like a vast tapeworm, slithering through the gut of England. The day is breaking over the English Channel, the crumbling chalk of Albion disintegrating flake by flake. Do we, the banished, still love this loveless land? I cannot say. When my lorry eventually loads onto the ferry and I stand with a steaming cup of bad coffee, staring back at the weird island of Brytania, as we say in Poland, I won't know what to think, I won't know what to feel. Am I ever coming back? Will I be welcome, or at least, not more unwelcome, when I return? We bring you all that you wish, after all, and we take away all that you sell. We carry everything you could possibly need. But we are only the messengers, only the tradesmen, only the vital connectors to the world beyond.

But why let thoughts rush ahead? We've hours of idle stagnation ahead of us. Hours to contemplate and to try and stop contemplating. Only those who can endure the constant chatter of doubt and distraction can drive these great engines of commerce. We have too much time, as we move and as we stall. Too much time to dream and regret.

Invisible Woman
by Claire Joyce

Shortlisted for the Edinburgh Award for Flash Fiction 2021

Sexless, ageless.
Female, mid 30s.

Colourless.
Dark brown hair, fair skin.

Voiceless.
Speaks with a strong Dublin accent.

Chameleon, will-o'-the-wisp, shape-shifting every-woman.
Medium build.

Reader, writer, dreamer, carer, secret-keeper, poetry speaker.
Unemployed.

Cat whisperer, bird feeder, bee protector, flower tender, butterfly spotter, stray adopter.
Socially isolated.

Rain dancer, puddle splasher, night-time stroller, starlight gazer, earworm hummer, sandwich sharer, finger tapper, leaf collector.
Mental health issues.

Street wanderer, people watcher, canal-bank sunbather, library lover, shop front shelterer, pavement dweller.
No fixed abode.

London ... Paris ... Milan ... New York ... Moscow ... Sydney ...
Last seen in Dublin's north inner city.

Fashion follower, hair curler, fingernail painter, funky hat wearer, handbag carrier, jewellery hoarder, scarf wrapper, shoe craver, colour clasher.
Possibly wearing black jeans and a dark top.

Thumb sucker, skin cutter, pain number, over eater, under eater, high achiever, attention seeker, people pleaser, late night screamer.
Comes from a respectable family background.

Punch receptor, head wrecker, bone crusher, nose bleeder, baby loser, no-good user, man hater, heart breaker, money scrounger, STUPID FUCKING WHORE!
No identifying scars.

Solace seeker. Canal bed sleeper.
Missing.

Free.
Presumed dead.

Inside Oot
by Angela Robb

Shortlisted, Scottish Arts Club Short Story Competition 2021

I'd hae stopped short ae killin the bastart, but Murray had other ideas.

I mean, I knew fae the start that Murray wis fuckin crazy. We met at thon support group for folk who've been in and oot the jile mair times than they can remember: Doin' Time and Time Again. We were an hour intae the session when Murray showed up: first time at the group, fresh oot the clanger for a serious assault, yellin fae the back ae the room, 'Awright lads! Hoo's it gaun?' He sat doon and said, 'Name's Murray,' and then the pish jist flowed fae his lips like it wis episode wan ae The Murray Show. I couldnae help starin – he had this thick scar ower his left eye and I couldnae figure oot how the hell there wis still an eye there in the middle ae it. They were icy blue, his eyes, and he wis short and fat and balding.

I wis too busy starin tae take in whit he wis sayin, but then, he wis too busy talkin shite tae take any notice ae me. There were a lot ae broken bottles and broken faces involved, I know that much. And he always seemed tae be the wan dealin them oot, in spite ae that scar. I finally tuned in the moment he shut up. He wis probably jist drawin breath; but Mike, the group leader, butted in quick and said, 'All right, welcome to the group and, eh, thanks for sharing. Janet – would you like to carry on?'

I sat there quietly till it wis ma turn, then updated them on how I'd been *managing my kleptomaniac tendencies* by wearing ma 'Stop me: I am a thief' sweater when I wis gaun tae the shops. I didnae mention that I'd had it on inside oot. But Murray. Murray looked at me wi this wee smirk, like he saw right through me.

Right then, I knew: he wisnae here tae mend his ways. He wis here tae find an accomplice.

When the session finished, I dodged outside quick as I could. But minutes later he caught up wi me at the bus stop. 'Awright there, Lenny! It is Lenny, in't it?'

'Aye, ye're right enough.'

He bent backwards and looked up at me, like he wis makin a joke aboot ma height. 'Can I call ye Lanky Lenny?' He laughed.

'Well ...'

'Right, let's cut tae the chase, Lanky Lenny. A leopard disnae turn ower a new leaf – neither dae I and neither dae you. So listen up, before yer fuckin bus comes.'

He telt me his proposition. I knew he wis a fuckin maniac, but then, I've a few bad habits masel.

We stood across the street fae the primary school. It wis a pissin wet filthy mornin, but that suited us fine. We could keep wir hoods up withoot lookin suspicious and folk were hurryin aboot wi their heids doon, oblivious tae the pair ae us.

The lollipop man did his thing, seein the weans safely across the road. Murray had been follaein him and knew where he lived.

'Five minutes' walk fae here tae Mister Lollipop's hoose,' said Murray.

A minute later I clocked a big fuck-off Mercedes comin fae the right and felt Murray tuggin ma sleeve. 'That's him!' he said.

The motor wis silver, wi wan ae thae private registration numbers: GE0FF 1, or something like that. 'Eight forty-seven, every mornin,' said Murray. 'Ma guy's got the phony plates and he's ready tae spray it and aw.'

'He's repaintin it?'

'Aye. Electric Tomato.'

'Whit?'

'The colour. Electric Tomato.'

Ma face screwed up ae its ain accord, but Murray went, 'Sshh!' and stuck his haund up. The lollipop man had nae customers, so the Merc cruised on by. I could make oot a wee man wi specs at the wheel.

'Right,' said Murray, still watchin efter the car. 'We all clear on whit we're daein then?'

'Aye,' I said. Because I really thought we were all clear.

But when we met in the lollipop man's street the next mornin, Murray said this:

'Awright. So we take care ae Lollipop, then when Geoff comes along in the Merc—'

'Geoff?'

'Aye. Did ye no read his number plate?'

'Aw aye.'

'Right. Geoff comes along in the Merc; ye stop him, weans or no weans. I turn on the Murray Charm – persuade him he's better aff on the pavement – you hop in the driver's seat and we bugger off oot ae it.'

Something wisnae quite right. 'Eh – how am I gettin in the driver's seat? I cannae drive. Well, I've got ma provisional licence—'

'Whit d'ye mean ye cannae drive?' Murray wis lookin at me like I'd ripped his knittin. 'Everyone drives!'

'Well I don't ... legally speakin. I took it *you* were drivin.'

'I cannae drive either!'

Fuckin idiot.

So we had tae improvise. First part ae the plan wis a piece ae piss: the lollipop man stepped oot his front door, Murray jumped him, knocked him oot wi a knuckleduster and dragged him back intae his hallway. I got his uniform aff him and we hurried round tae the school. The big yellow jaiket droont me and the waterproof troosers stopped haufwey up ma calves.

I pulled the cap doon ower ma face when the first ae the kids showed up. 'Over yese go,' I telt them and that wis me in the swing ae things. Ma timing wisnae great and there were a few emergency stops, but seriously, it wis the easiest fuckin job ever.

'I should be gettin paid for this,' I shouted at Murray, but jist then the silver Merc came intae view. I stood on the white line wi ma lollipop and the car slowed tae a stop. I could see the wee man starin at me through the windscreen: there were nae kids.

Murray pulled a balaclava ower his heid, bounced aff the pavement and opened the driver's door. I wisnae surprised tae see he had a knife.

'Awright Geoff! This is a carjacking, Geoff. Now since neither myself nor my associate possess a full UK driving licence, you're gonnae dae the drivin. Got it?'

He shut the driver's door and opened the back yin, jerkin his heid at me as he got in. I wis aboot tae run forward when a couple ae kids appeared at the kerb.

'Eh ... over yese go.'

They daunered across the road and I couldnae help meetin Geoff's glaikit stare before I remembered I wis supposed tae be hidin ma face. I tugged ma cap doon.

'I said GO!'

The kids gied me a dirty look but hurried on tae the pavement. I ran tae the back door ae the car and I wis still tryin tae manoeuvre masel and ma lollipop inside when Murray sterted shoutin, 'GO, GEOFF, GO!!'

We seemed tae crawl aw the wey oot ae the city and on tae the country roads. Or mibbie that's jist how it felt, wi Murray gassin on aboot how Geoff better no get any clever ideas.

We were oot in the arse end ae nowhere when Murray telt Geoff tae stop the car.

'Get oot,' said Murray.

48

'What for?' Geoff sounded irritated.

'Jist dae it,' I advised.

So we aw got oot and Murray pointed across the fields and said, 'There's yer way back, Geoff. We're gonnae call our guy tae come and collect the motor, you're gonnae hotfoot it across aw that grass. Cannae have ye walkin on the road and clypin tae anybody that comes along now, can we? Aw, and gie us yer phone obviously.'

Geoff sighed, but haunded ower the phone. 'This is what I get for sending you down, is it Murray?'

Murray froze. 'How d'ye know ma name?'

Now it wis Geoff's turn tae look rattled. 'I'd know that piercing stare and daft bravado anywhere.' The colour drained fae his face. 'You don't recognise me?' Murray shook his head. 'Then how did you know *ma* name?'

'Yer number plate.'

'Aw, that.'

Geoff wis lookin at his number plate like it might jist be the biggest mistake he'd ever made. Murray said nothin for at least ten seconds, but whit wis even mair amazin wis how much ye could see his face screw up despite the balaclava.

'You *bastard*,' he said, quietly. Geoff jumped. 'Geoffrey Whittock QC, but withoot the wee wig. Whit wis it ye called me again?'

'I … um …'

' "A pathetic small-time thug masquerading as a hardman. Find this man guilty, ladies and gentlemen," ye said, "for the good ae us all." Well it hasnae done *you* much good, Geoff…' Murray reached intae the car and pulled oot the lollipop. 'I can tell ye that for nothin.'

Geoff pit his haunds up and sterted tae back away. He didnae get far. Murray swung the lollipop like a fuckin baseball bat and there wis a *smack* mixed wi a *crunch*. Geoff drapped tae the ground wi his neck aw twistit.

We stood ower him. 'Is he deid?' I asked.

'Aye, of course he's deid.'

'And wis that really necessary?'

Murray yanked the balaclava aff his heid and glared at me. 'Ye heard whit the wee prick called me!' His voice jumped an octave. 'And he *knew who I wis!*'

'True.'

'Come on, let's get him oot the wey.' Murray lifted Geoff under the armpits. 'You take the feet.'

'I'd rather no touch him, if it's aw the same.'

Murray stared. 'For fuck's sake,' he said, then he pulled Geoff tae the fence, scrambled ower it and dragged the body between the wires. '*Masquerading*, am I Geoff?' he asked, as he and the QC disappeared behind the hedgerow. 'Hardman enough for ye now?'

I chewed ma lip. Then I pit the lollipop on the back seat, climbed intae the driver's seat and turned on the engine. The Merc wis an automatic, which wis very helpful. By the time Murray appeared in ma rear-view mirror, wavin his fists and screamin, I wis glidin along at thirty mile an hour doon the middle ae the road.

'I'm a *kleptomaniac*, ya daft bastart!'

And the thing aboot bein wan ae them is that I'm compelled tae steal but dinnae gie a fuck aboot financial gain. So I gripped the steering wheel and flung the Merc round aw thae twisty bends and eventually found ma wey back tae the city. I bounced aff the kerb a few times and probably missed a red light or two, but I pulled intae the car park at the polis station withoot puttin a scratch on the motor.

At the trial, Murray pit on quite a show. That wis the first I realised Murray wisnae his surname. *Murray Maxwell*. Sounds like a Tory MSP. I thought he might plead guilty tae show the prosecution whit a hardman he wis, but he protested his innocence wi this weird, whiny persona like he wis a poor wee small-time thug gettin picked on. But the ladies and gentlemen of the jury knew a fuckin psycho when they saw one and he went doon for a minimum ae twenty.

As for me, well, haundin masel in and tellin all got me a nice lenient sentence for ma crimes ae assault and robbery, posing as a school crossing patrol officer, grand theft auto, kidnapping and driving unsupervised on a provisional licence. I have tae say I felt fair chuffed at havin helped take a murderous wanker aff the streets, even if I'd also helped bring aboot the murder. And it felt good tae be back in the jile, tae be honest. The guards were like mates and I'd been missin them.

Now I'm oot early for good behaviour, on condition that I go back tae the support group and try harder this time. So I go along every week and tell everyone how I've been wearin ma stop-me-I'm-a-thief sweater as a symbol ae how I want tae live ma life. Inside, oot.

Pulled
by Kitty Waldron

Shortlisted for the Edinburgh Award for Flash Fiction 2021

Met him in a bar and he was stunning although he was knitted. OK, don't judge me, but we slept together. He got up before me and made me tea and toast with crunchy peanut butter cut into triangles.

He came around the next night and we enjoyed a Chinese takeaway with crispy seaweed while watching *Muriel's Wedding*.

He made me tea, but toast with just butter. Oh. Maybe he's not quite so well-knitted as I thought. There's a thread just coming loose.

The next night, jacket potato, cheese and beans. We watched *Sewing Bee*. But then he was very critical of Joe Lycett. Oh, that thread. I just gave it a little tug.

He forgot to put a teabag in the hot water, so it was just a mug of hot water and a piece of toast.

Then we had to watch *Monster Trucks*. I had no interest in this so I spent the whole episode pulling on that thread. It was immensely satisfying.

Next it was *Fast and Furious*. He barely spoke to me all evening. We got an Indian and he wouldn't share his peshwari naan. He's falling apart at the seams.

What the hell! Who the heck orders double capers? And *Fast and Furious 5*? He isn't hard to pull apart.

I had to get up to make myself a cup of tea. I followed a trail of wool downstairs and it ended at the kettle. No man in sight. Our relationship had unravelled.

When Ioannis's goat got out
by Michael Toolan

Shortlisted, Scottish Arts Club Short Story Competition 2021

The day we learned that Ioannis Chloros's billy goat had got out and couldn't be found the village was both outraged and delighted. Outraged at the owner's irresponsibility: think of the damage to property the animal could do, not to mention interfering with other people's females. But delighted too, because in a place like this you crave any news; the days can be awful long otherwise. Marios finally agreed a price with the Ganoulises for the field that was never much use to him; Eleni-Maria had her knee operation and'll be home by the weekend; the council have filled in that horrible hole out on the Agiassos road. That sort of thing. It's something to chew over sitting outside companionably with your neighbours in the long autumn evenings. Something to shout back and forth about in Kostas's bar nursing your one glass of ouzo. Any snippet is pounced on and squeezed dry through talk, talk, talk. And what better than an absconding billy goat? Especially one with a name. Yes, Ioannis had given him his own name: Yaki!

It was Dimitra who first alerted everyone to the calamity, not Ioannis himself – well, he was too proud or embarrassed I suppose. And she being one of his nearer neighbours, she would have been one of the first he visited, asking if she'd seen hide or hair of your man Yaki. She had not, but must have felt some sympathy for the frustrated creature: she volunteered to get the word out and see if the animal couldn't be tracked down, found grazing on someone's fig trees perhaps, or happy as Larry working his way through the carefully-planted flower garden of some civil servant, holidays over, now back in Athens.

Living on her own since her husband died of that cruel disease, their only child settled and married in Pennsylvania, Dimitra knew a thing or two about losing what you value most. A fine-looking woman was Dimitra, then as now, a powerful mane of thick black hair down to her muscular shoulders, her eyes two liquid brown pools, and a body to set the poets singing. Any man on the island would have been proud to walk out with her, only she showed no inclination to take up with anyone after her beloved Michalis passed away.

As for that animal away on his unauthorised odyssey – 'Yaki' indeed – he was cute alright. I remember looking him in the face, the time Ioannis brought him over to serve our dams. Looking into those eyes with the vertical black unblinking pupils, his long, bony skull and Ho Chi Minh beard, and wondering if he knew what a good time he was in for. But he never gave anything away, smart enough to know that if he looked stupid, you'd think he was stupid. Fifteen years old according to Ioannis (nearer twenty, I reckoned), weighing as much as a man, a thick cream-and-brown fur courtesy of his wild ancestors, strong haunches on him and plenty of seed in his swaying sack to supply all the ladies brought to him. Valuable, then: the most valuable thing Ioannis owned, after the smallholding itself.

Every time anyone asked Ioannis how it could have happened, he told how Yaki had been so quiet the previous weeks, hardly moving a few feet to graze in the course of an afternoon, that he'd decided he didn't have to bell him. And he needed a spare bell, until he got around to buying one in town, to put on the extra nanny he had kept back to breed from. A bit slap-dash like that was Ioannis, if he thought he could get away with it.

So that's how he came to remove the billy-goat's bell. But without that bell to alert him, Ioannis was none the wiser – slept soundly on – the night Yaki took it upon himself to slip away by the light of a waxing moon, probably having to gird his loins and make a wee jump to get up and over the low point in the stone wall that Ioannis had also been meaning to fix for months. And then away down the monopati, across that plot of scrubland thick with heather and thorny knapweed that a teacher from the mainland had bought and only put concrete footings for a house on so far, and off with him God knows where. Up the valley, down the valley, who could say? The village wags had a field day. One thought he might have headed for the Axiotissa restaurant, offering himself up, a month's worth of extra-tough *katsiki lemonato*. Another said he was seen at the port late one afternoon, lining up with everyone else to take the Blue Star ferry back to the capital: a business trip! But it was no laughing matter for Ioannis, who clenched his fists and yelled blood and violence when such levity reached his ears.

A tough old goat himself, was Ioannis. He must have been sixty or near it then, living alone for a decade, ever since Panagiota had upped and left him. A surly uncommunicative fellow, not over-keen on a wash or a shave, with worn-down yellowing teeth more often seen in a grimace than a smile. They had started out well enough, he and Panagiota, a delicate-featured woman from a family settled in the main town of the island, with a fondness for books and nice clothes: she was suited to life in a town or better yet a city, not up a lonely track in the sun-baked back of beyond. But when their two lovely girls finished high school and turned cool towards the local boys, announcing they were heading for the capital in search of office jobs, it knocked all the happiness and point out of Ioannis's life. And didn't it show.

He became withdrawn in company, started blaming his wife for their daughters' fancy notions as he called them, their 'disloyalty'. The two lights in his life were leaving them, leaving him, and the imaginings that must have been sustaining him through the chill unproductive winters, the burning summers – toiling from sunup to sundown for the meagre profits earned from his livestock and crops and hives – were all crushed. His dreams of retiring with the farmhouse extended and renovated by two salaried and respectful sons-in-law, surrounded by — what? five, maybe six or seven! – grandchildren, three women to make his meals and do his washing and drive him into town (both families would own an air-conditioned car by then wouldn't they?) … all shattered like a carelessly dropped amphora. She had let them break up the family, he would shout at her and shout a lot more besides. An animal in pain. He never laid a hand on her, as far as we knew, but he must have been a torment to live with.

Plenty of our women used to put up with that sort of thing; what option had they? So the blow must have been all the greater when a year later she told him she was going to the capital for a week, to see their girls' apartment for herself, and to see the kind of people they were socialising with (she meant their men friends). And never came back. His face grew long and lined, his beard grey and neglected, his shoulders stooped from walking with eyes downcast. He'd pass you on the road without acknowledgement, sometimes muttering to himself. Eccentric: yes, I'd say he became a bit eccentric.

And Dimitra, what can you say about Dimitra, who had been such close friends with Panagiota? I'm not sure she helped, marching up to Ioannis the first time he showed his face in town on market day, about six months after the wife had left him and started the divorce process. Telling him it was his own fault, he was a bloody fool and stubborn as a mule. He had two lovely daughters and their going off to make their own lives didn't change that; and now his grumpiness had driven Pana away too, her dearest friend! Tears were in her eyes as she turned on her heel and strode off towards her battered pick-up, the gawping idle ones scattering to let her through.

Well, after all that, who should it be but Dimitra herself who came to the rescue, solved the mystery. After she went into town specially and Giorgos-the-police laughed off her request for help, she put the word out that all Yaki sightings or 'evidence' should be reported to her, preferably by phone. The following weeks she methodically marked these reports, the plausible and the unlikely, on a map. In time she noticed the bulk of them suggested the fugitive was moving away from home along one of the greener – less bone-dry at least – valleys. Leaving behind the oregano and thyme of the hills, the juniper and the mastic bushes, he seemed to be working his way through the softer-leaved garrigue scrubland towards the coast. Inspired by the hikers, perhaps.

She hit the jackpot when taking her niece Efthymia – a student away in Thessaloniki most of the year – to the beach one late afternoon. Unusually she picked a beach favoured by the nudist foreigners. They liked it for being secluded but with some shade too, from compact tamarisks sustained by a stream that trickled most of the year down the same valley where there'd been reported sightings of Yaki.

According to Efthymia, they hadn't got far from Dimitra's truck, parked in a bed of soft sand, when they came across Yaki, identifiable by his broad backside and nonchalantly-displayed masculinity. All balls and no bell, you might say. They made a fine picture, Yaki and the nudists. While the humans sat facing the glittering, ever-moving sea in devout and mesmerized contemplation, Yaki was turned in the opposite direction, snapping and crunching his way through every scrap of unappetizing vegetation within his reach. Not that the nude sunbathers were as tolerant of him as he them. That animal looked like it would try to eat anything left unprotected, and the men in

57

particular feared for their understandably shrinking bits. At any rate, they gave Yaki a wide berth, spending longer in the sea than usual, taking turns to keep watch on the goat's progress. Surprise combined with relief, therefore, when they witnessed someone who was clearly a local woman approach the billy purposefully and slap a noose around his neck and lead him calmly back to her pickup.

Next thing we knew, not only was Ioannis reunited with his blasted goat, he'd also managed to tether the fine Dimitra, as handsome a woman as ever baked bread around here. Or, unlikely as it would seem, maybe it was she who tethered him, having weighed up her other prospects, assessing the true heft and cut of the man. Maybe they spat on their hands and clapped them together in a deal, how would I know?

Of course, that was all a good five years ago. And now Ioannis has even less time for his goats. You can see him every weekday morning, walking down from his farm to the kindergarten in the village, loosely yoked to his two lovely four-year-olds by that rope the teacher recommends. And back to the house with them again at lunchtime. And plenty of chat with all and sundry along the way, a grin on his face like a melon slice. Twins! At his age, imagine! The Lord is good.

And so this particular tragedy ends happily. Would you credit it? Nothing as queer as folk; unless it's goats. Some say Dimitra had the whole thing planned out, from start to finish; others say that that bloody goat knows a lot more than he's letting on. A few killjoys say don't always be over-interpreting everything, like there has to be a moral in it or something.

I Love You
by Meg MacLeod

Shortlisted for the Edinburgh Award for Flash Fiction 2021

He stood in the dock. Guilty. Unanimous. She was shocked, not at the verdict, but at herself. She had loved him for 15 years, loved his quiet attentiveness, his attention to detail.

It was the detail that trapped him. Neatly tied with the same twine he used to stake the peas, the five little packages in the potting shed were a gift to the detectives; shades of blonde hair clippings, his precious mementos.

All the time in court he had looked straight ahead. Only when he was taken down did he glance at her. He mouthed the words, 'I love you'.

The years unravelled backwards to the beginning. He said he liked brunettes. Was this the reason she was still alive? Were all her years with him balanced on a precipice? How long would it take her to understand? She stopped her thoughts. Hands shaking now, she made coffee and watched the news reporting the court case. Friends had stepped away. She couldn't blame them.

Detectives had searched the house. There was nothing untouched. There was nothing decent left, nothing left of their sacred vows.

She went to the glass-screened visitors room with one question, 'Why?'

He cried, like the child they never had, 'I don`t know'.

She burnt their bed and his possessions. She kept the silver locket with the picture of his mother, a pretty blonde woman with eyes as cold as ice. It was, she thought, inside this locket that she would find the answer.

Fading footsteps
by John Coughlan

Longlisted, Scottish Arts Club Short Story Competition 2021

I was nine that Christmas of nineteen forty-four. The weather was hard in New Galloway, a foot of crisp snow on the ground and a biting frost. The drinking fountain in the school playground had frozen and James Nesbit licked it and stuck his tongue. The hills and the woods looked like a picture called *Hoar Frost* that hung over the fireplace. We'd been bombed out of Nan's house in Douglas Street during the Clydebank Blitz and she went to stay with her sister in Maryhill.

Mum and I went to New Galloway where my other nan and granpop farmed at The Mullet. Mum worked in the canteen at the flying boat base at Portpatrick and I helped around the farm before school, after school and at weekends. We grew beets and cabbages and potatoes and kept some beasts. Dairy cows, some pigs and chickens and a flock of hill sheep. We had two giant Clydesdale horses named Hector and Achilles. Granpop said tractors were smelly soulless things, no heart.

It was hard, but we were better off than most that fourth year of war. Granpop said it would soon be over as the Yanks were come to save us, always late. Best of all was a telegram from Dad saying he'd be home for two days over Christmas. That night I sat by the window watching for him as the snow piled deeper against the hedge. Granpop came to watch with me, lit his old pipe and put a lighted candle in the window to guide Dad.

'Will my daddy get home, Granpop, with all this snow; he will, won't he?'

He tussled my hair. 'He'll come like Shackleton with huskies if need be. Come help me oil the harness and read

Jungle Book.'

No huskies came but Dad got a lift from an RAF lorry. Mum held him and couldn't speak.

She just hugged him, laughed a little and cried a lot, touching his face and hiding hers in the rough serge of his greatcoat. When I asked Gran what was the matter with Mum, she shooshed me and took me into the kitchen. Mum asked him how long and when he told her Boxing Day, she started to cry again. I thought it funny she should cry, because Dad was home and not dead like Russell MacKay's dad, who would not ever be home again. Women are funny that way.

That night we all sat in the glow of the range and I had Horlicks in a tin mug from Dad's pack. The men had whisky from a dusty bottle concealed deep in the sideboard. Dad told me stories about Africa, Italy and Normandy, all the places he had seen. I thought how lucky he was and told him I would be a soldier when I grew up. He looked sad and ruffled my hair. Gran whispered, "God forbid!" and crossed herself. I fell asleep on Dad's knee after my Horlicks and he carried me to my bed under the stair.

Mum and Dad were still not up when I came down for breakfast Christmas Eve morning, but when I knocked on their door Gran scolded me and chased me out to help Grandad with the cows. When I finished my porridge Dad was up and had on his old working clothes from before the war. He said we would harrow the lower field today and I rushed out to fetch Achilles and Hector. Placid as lambs they lowered their heads for the halter and I led them down to where Dad waited. I asked him why we were harrowing in the winter, in the snow. He hunkered down, deftly attaching harness and clip and stared down to where the trees were pink and white in the weak sun.

'I may not be home in the Spring. It's best done now.'

He fell silent and I took his hand, barely caught his

61

whisper.

'I know it's daft but I need to do something normal. To feel the earth.'

He sat on the metal seat and I climbed up behind him, my arms around his neck. He cracked the reins and whistled. We spent a useless morning lulled by the jingle of harness and the solid metronomic thumps of giant hooves. Dad sucked on his old pipe while I perched behind him on my clanking chariot, proud as any Caesar.

That night we sat around the wireless in the best room, talking and making paper decorations. Grandad had a tree from the forest at the back and we fixed it up with the lights and paper streamers and it looked just lovely. Dad let me help him use the metal snips to cut up empty tins into star shapes. Mum kept touching Dad and kissing him. Every time they passed, they would cuddle and later they both got giggly on the 'stuff' that Grandad kept in the barn. Mum sat on his knee and they kissed and cuddled right there in front of everybody. I thought it was really soppy. Later we went to midnight mass, the first time for me. We put the Tilley lamps on poles, Dad hoisted me on his shoulders and waded through the snow.

The church was candlelit, the stained-glass windows reflecting the candles people had brought. By the door was the crib with cardboard figures we'd painted at school. People brushed the snow off their coats by the door and a rainbow puddle formed, it's surface rippling in the coloured light. My best pal Russell was there with his mum who was crying. In the choir stall was the organist Mrs Fairbairn, whose two older boys were dead somewhere in Italy. Her choir was a mix of local children plus Italian and German POW's. Silent night was in three languages all at once, a bit like the Tower of Babel. Some of the Italians wept and I didn't think they could have killed the Fairbairn boys, or Russell's dad. A lot of people came up to speak to my dad and I was really proud sitting with the men at the back of the church hall later. Dad tall and straight in his uniform, his red beret and ribbons glowing in the lamplight.

Christmas morning the cold woke me under the stair. A huge woollen sock lay by the side of the bed which I grabbed and charged into the kitchen shouting, 'Santa's been, Santa's been.' before spilling my stocking across the kitchen table which had an orange and a Hershey bar with a brand new *Victor* comic. Under the tree was a toy aeroplane and a book, *The Man in the Iron Mask*. There was a red torch with batteries, a heavy wool pullover from Gran and lots of chocolate from Dad. As a reward for all the help I had been to him, Grandad gave me his second-best penknife. That was a surprise as he never seemed to do anything but complain and humph about me. It had two blades and a bottle opener.

Dinner was a like a Roman feast. We had goose and potatoes and jelly and chocolate cake and fizzy lemonade Mum had made with the sugar ration. I was glad we ate the goose as it used to chase and nip me in the yard. After dinner we listened to the King. Mum sang a silly song called *The Inversneckie Store* and Dad sang *Lili Marlene* in German. I ate a huge slab of the Hershey bar and was sick in glorious colours over the range. Cleaned up, I got to sit on Dad's knee later and we sang and played charades, but most of all I just snuggled into his chest and fell asleep listening to Christmas carols on the wireless.

I have a drowsy memory of him kneeling by the mattress tucking me into the dunny bed under the stair. He seemed to stand there a long time as if reluctant to leave me and I came awake later to see him still by my bed. I smiled and mumbled, 'what are you looking at, Dad?'

'Just you son, just you,' he said softly, kissing me and tucking the quilt under my chin. 'Filling my eyes with you.' I giggled and thought how silly that was, how could he fill his eyes with me?

Boxing Day morning we were all up early. Dad had to be in Stranraer for the train by nine so he'd arranged a lift on the dairy lorry along with the milk churns. Mum cried all morning as she moved around and Dad kept touching her gently and holding her hand. By the door sat his kitbag and pack. The clock on the kitchen mantle struck the hour and Dad stood up. Mum made a small cry like a new-born lamb and both hands flew to her mouth. Nobody said anything as he put on his coat and gear, except Granny, who gibbered nonsense about keeping warm and dry and coming home safe. Nan and Papa took me outside to wait so I grabbed the last piece of soda bread.

The fog was down from the hill, clinging to the trees dripping and freezing in the watery sun. My balaclava was hard with my runny nose. Dad came out. He looked funny, like the boys at school when they fell off the railing wall and didn't want to cry in front of everyone.

Gran hugged him and told him to write soon. Grandad shook his hand and they just nodded to each other.

'Dad.'

'Son.'

'See you soon.'

'Aye.'

Dad put his hand on my head and held my face up then took my hand and drew me down the path to the gate. The fog nearly hid the house twenty feet away. He crouched down to me grasping both my arms.

'I want you to be a good boy and look after your mum for me.'

I nodded, not fully understanding, fighting my own tears. He seemed at a loss what to say next, as if he had something really important to tell me but didn't know where to start. I put my arms around his neck.

'Will you be home soon Dad, forever?'

64

He held me so tight I couldn't breathe. He stood up and took off his wristwatch, the American pilot's one. 'Here! you're the man off the house for now, you'll be needing a watch to keep your Mum right.'

I was shocked to see my dad was crying.

He turned and marched off, his boots crunching in the snow. At the corner he turned and looked back at me, waved and smiled, then turned and strode into the fog. It swallowed him and I stood staring after him listening to his footsteps fading away till there was only silence.

My parents look at me now from the photograph on the kitchen mantle; myself on Dad's shoulders, all of us smiling hugely from that happy time long ago, when I was a little boy. My sons help me on the farm now, their children in my place. Hector and Achilles are long gone, the stable a tractor shed. Grandad was right, a tractor has no heart. The watch still keeps good time and Grandad's knife is in my pocket, blade honed thin and the handle smooth from use.

Standing here by the gate, as I have every Boxing Day morning since then and remember him, I have at last come to understand the many things he wanted to tell me and why he was crying. Gazing up the road, my eyes are tight shut against the tears, my heart is bursting.

His coat is rough against my cheek and his arms tight about me.

My ears echo still with his crunching footsteps fading into the fog.

And my eyes?

My eyes are filled with his going.

Drowning Lifeguard
by Peter Lomax

Shortlisted for the Edinburgh Award for Flash Fiction 2021

I'm sitting on my white wooden seat on top of a stepladder watching the bathers splashing below me like a peregrine looking for prey, armed with my whistle to impale any excess teenage exuberance. Hot enough to be comfortable in swimming costumes, in here the Edinburgh winter feels like summer in my home city of Aleppo.

Despite my perched vigilance, in this heat my mind often strays to the Syrian pre-war days with friends swimming in the Mediterranean, the races at the Assad pool and time spent playing in Aleppo's waterways. The friends now either dead or dispersed, the Med beaches now covered in landmines, the pool drained and waterways full of bodies.

To qualify as a lifeguard involved exams in a language I barely knew. My old qualifications reduced to dust like my home and family. But still authorities ask to see certificates that no longer exist, a passport which is no longer readable or references from people no longer alive.

The job application filled me with terror.

Swimming experience? Do I include the overnight escape swimming from Turkey to Greece?

Travel? Would they like to know about the hours clinging to the underside of trucks?

But now, despite all the efforts to rebuild a life, I am drowning. Pockets weighed down by the concrete letter from a home office administrator telling me I must leave this life that has been so hard to establish and return to the war-torn divided ruins of my former home.

The Errand
by Jacob Palley

Longlisted, Scottish Arts Club Short Story Competition 2021

Everything hung in the air that day. The cold, omnipresent and oppressive, cut right to the bone. The one child who braved the outdoors felt it immediately. Each step brought one new breath of air, each exhalation resulting in a tiny poof of white ice as the moisture froze upon contact with the outside world. With no wind, each breath stayed in suspended animation and hovered exactly where the boy left it, as if by magic. If it did not feel like his neck would freeze into place if he turned it, the kid would have had the time to look back to see that the sun sparked off each one, creating a translucent, golden glimmer.

The cold creeped into all of his body and he had to stay focused. His head started to ache; his teeth began to chatter. The protective layers of wool around his hands seemed entirely inadequate. He thrust his hands – they felt more like wooden paddles at this point – deeper into his pockets and moved around his fingers to fight off the inevitable frostbite. His shoes squeaked against the grey, compacted snow left from the snowstorm that blew through last week. He shivered at the sound of it and picked up his pace. It would be at least another mile to the store.

The sun did no favours. Its rays fell impotently to the surface, defeated by a presence so chilling that the vacuum of space felt warm by comparison. As the boy ran across the high plains towards the store, the sun made a slow dance over him running the opposite direction, flatly illuminating each puff of air the boy left behind.

He arrived at the store just as the sun began to meet the horizon, setting the sky ablaze in a cacophony of yellow, orange and purples. He wasn't supposed to have arrived this late into the day, but the weather had dragged him down, set him back. The temperature plunged further as darkness crept in all around him.

The faster he had moved, the warmer he had felt. Now, the sweat his body had accumulated from the trek betrayed him. He felt the beads draining the heat from his core and knew they would turn to ice if he did not get indoors soon. He took one last breath and then pushed on the store's door. He kept pushing until the door – sealed by the ice that had accumulated around its wooden frame – finally cracked and gave way. The door opened with a whoosh and then with a bang as it swung at a full clip into the wall and then he came inside.

Heat. So much heat. The feeling returned first to his toes and his fingers and the ice crystals that formed on his brow and eyelashes started to melt off. The cathartic yet painful sensation of having feeling return to one's extremities is both wonderful and disorienting. The boy stood there, revelling in it. Then suddenly from behind the counter, "Close that door, Jack! You know better than to leave it open. Heat ain't free, you know?"

The boy shook his head and came to his senses and immediately closed the door. He had been standing in the store for who knows how long and suddenly the rows of provisions above the storekeep's head snapped into focus. So too did the roaring fire off to his right. The fire felt like it had enveloped the store, conquering the cold to the point where if you looked at the windows, the heat radiating out from the fire met the icicles penetrating in from the outside, their sharp, pointy ends aiming directly at the boy's heart. The fire and ice apparently battled at the windowpane; a pool of melted water formed along the windowsill.

The boy and the storekeep locked eyes on each other. "So, what do you want? The usual provisions, I'm guessing?" The boy nodded. "It's dreadful outside. Why don't you stay by the fire as I get everything packaged up for you? Nobody has been here all day on account of the weather, so it's not like I don't have the time!" Even if he had wanted to say something in reply, his jaw still felt frozen shut. He shuffled to the fire and began to dry himself out and warm himself up. He looked to the window and saw that the fire and the ice continued to do battle, the atrocities of their war playing out with each drop of water slowly hitting the floor. There would be no truce between them today.

The storekeep yelled from the back, "I checked the temperature an hour ago but the mercury completely froze. Will you make it back OK? I think you can, so long as you dry out all your clothes and heat them up as much as you can before you head out!" The boy nodded, knowing that he never truly needed to answer. The storekeep always answered his own questions.

"You know what else you need? Moonshine. It came in from the town over. See that your dad gets it – that ain't for fellas like yourself. Even one drop of the stuff will set you alight!"

The provisions, now ready to go, sat next to the door in a tightly-wound package. "Things look different at night, makes it harder to get back. In case you forget …" The storekeep snapped his fingers. "I've got just the thing!" He took a piece of coal as dark and as thick as the night sky and used it to draw a map for the boy right on the brown paper he used to wrap up the provisions. The store looked like a small house, the boy's house marked with a huge X.

The distance he would have to traverse between the two felt tremendous even if the map represented the true distance he would have to travel between points A and B. Just a few inches of travel outside in the elements would be enough to make anyone cower at the thought. This boy would have to travel miles. The boy followed the thick black lines etched into the paper with his eyes and then had to turn away because they looked like they ran off into infinity.

The boy slowly, methodically, let his jacket and gloves and the rest of clothes soak in the heat from the fire. Once they glowed orange, he put each layer back on, basking in the radiance. "Atta boy, Jack! Who's the bravest kid I know? You are! You are." The boy nodded, smiling with his eyes. His jaw had defrosted itself for a long time now and was back to wrapping itself around the English lexicon, but he quickly determined that it was not needed at present. He tucked the package under his jacket and took one last deep breath of air.

"Are you ready to travel? You can only carry so much heat with you! Time to go, Jack!"

"You nearly froze us all out when you came through here before. I'm going to close that door as soon as I open it. Be ready, be *ready*!" The storekeep tried to push the door open with a finger. Then with his hand. Then with a fist. Then with the shoulder. The door would not budge. He went to the back, got the blowtorch and started to heat up the frame. Melted water began to gush down the sides. The storekeep again rammed his shoulder into the door and this time it swung wildly open to the outside world. The door struck the general store's façade, the force knocking off the icicles, which rained down like bombs and hit the snow with a thud. The wave of wind swept in and extinguished the fire. The boy was too focused to notice. He looked onwards, determined, and had already thrown himself across the threshold, steeling himself as the world turned black.

He knew from experience that the heat would start to dissipate. He had to keep momentum and had to make it home. His family depended on him getting the provisions safely back.

Visibility under the night sky was limited. The cold had locked everything into place and even the stars refused to come out, lest they too be extinguished by that oppressive

70

force. Yet he instinctively knew the direction home, keeping the package with the crudely scrawled map under his multiple layers and close to his heart. He could read the map better that way. He started to run into the night.

It happened so suddenly, there was no time to catch himself. His left foot hit something he hadn't fully seen in the shadows and his velocity carried him to such a pitch that it was his face that hit first, followed by his chest and then the rest of his body. The force of the impact shocked him, leaving him in a stupor. Worse, the impact forced the hot air out of his jackets, his layers of clothes, his only layers of protections. He felt like a balloon that had just been popped, seeping out the inside that kept him light, buoyant. The beads of sweat accumulating from his return journey began to ball up and they began to freeze. The shivering started anew. His provisions seemed to be in place, but he did not dare unzip his jacket to check.

He fought off the urge to panic. A wrong move here could mean the difference between life and death. His head was still spinning and he fought to get that under control first. He then felt his fingers, wiggled his toes, blinked and shook his head. The provisions, miraculously, had survived the fall, save one casualty. The bottle of moonshine lay on the ice, crushed and broken. Its liquid had spilled out, forming a silvery mess below.

He struggled to get up. He put one knee up and the other to the ground and then he touched his hands to the icy surface beneath him. He pushed down against the earth with his hands, throwing his body against the incontrovertible law of gravity, urging himself upwards.

He was finally standing, yet something was off. He no longer knew how to get back home. He could feel that the map that had been carefully etched into the brown paper was irreparably torn. He spun around like a compass without a magnetic north, unable to gain his sense of direction, unable to plot his course back home. With this realization, he again collapsed to the ground. The still air started to seep in from all angles, suffocating him. The panic turned to despair. He would never, ever make it home. He cried uncontrollably.

Lying now on his left side, he saw the puddle of moonshine burn off into the night sky. He shook his head, not believing his eyes. He looked up again and, when he did, he saw a full moon directly above him.

The moonlight began to dance off surfaces, breathing life into the stillness and back into the boy. And there, directly in front of him, floating like a sheet of gossamer was a breath of air he had expelled many hours ago into the daylight. The total stillness of the day had not just kept the delicate ice crystals intact but had locked into place exactly where he had blown each puff of air into existence. The crystals glittered faintly in the moonlight.

He looked again and saw an identical one close by, and then another and another and another, stretching off into the night, shimmering like a diamond bracelet against the black of night. The boy stood, his bearings now locked on the incandescent trail ahead of him, and his house just beyond that.

He took a deep breath, made sure his provisions were still wrapped under the jacket and close to his heart, and then sprinted off confidently into the night.

Short Straw
by Christina Eagles

Shortlisted for the Edinburgh Award for Flash Fiction 2021

Miriam and her friends are squealing outside. The sound calls me to the hot air of the open window where I can watch them crouched together in the dust. My stomach clenches when I see that they are drawing straws again. I've told her not to do that, but she looks at me blankly. What can I say? I know that for them it's only a fun way of choosing who will turn the handle of the skipping rope. There is no way to explain to my daughter what it once meant to me,

The night I drew the short straw from an outstretched hand that trembled, my mother begged to go in my place. But the others said no, she was too scrawny, too old. I listened to her weeping as I walked across the yard to the fair-haired men leaning on their rifles. I tried to hold my head high but I could feel the pee trickling hot down the insides of my thighs.

This morning, I breathe again when I see that it is not Miriam this time. One of the others steps back and shows what she holds. I watch the girls as they tie a scarf around her eyes and send her spinning at the centre of their circle.

It is always easy to pick out Miriam in the group. Against the black hair of her friends, hers shines, the colour of straw.

Vesper's Gift
by Alexandra Morton

Longlisted, Scottish Arts Club Short Story Competition 2021

I brought him an orange. We'd had fresh ones delivered that morning, ones with puckered navels that smelled of sun. The particular tilt of his expression made me wonder whether he had ever received such a token before. The arch of his brow asked for an explanation; was he not the one to be paying me? All the same, he drew a penknife from his waistcoat pocket. He exposed the flesh with a grimace and deposited the fragments of peel, cringing in their newfound state of separation, upon the long oak table. The tang of turpentine softened for a time.

I picked my way over the stoor-strewn hardwood and tried to give at least the appearance of grace. My mother would have taken a broom and pan to the place with just as much glee as disgust. Order was clearly reserved for his canvases.

A candle burned near his easel; its wick hunched over like a spine. It could only have been lit out of fancy, as he was the sort who had already had electricity installed. His folk were from up Bearsden way and could afford it, or so I had heard.

Waving his hand, he said I might find a robe behind the folding screen rammed in the far corner. I was to use it, if I so wished. The charade of preserving my modesty until the last possible moment was as amusing as it was absurd. Nevertheless, I swallowed the thought. I might have been new to the work, but I hadn't hesitated when he'd offered it. My father's broken arm had put him out of work since before Jim's birthday.

I had already schooled myself not to tremble, examining myself as thoroughly as I could through the distorting lens of my bathwater so as to identify in advance all that might be considered displeasing. I held my breath and imagined what it might be like for someone else to see me this way. Any confidence that I might have found in preparing so thoroughly evaporated as soon as the cool air surged against my bare shins.

And still ...

Shop girls like me sold soap and sugar and tea and made a tidy wage in exchange for sore hands and feet. But by then, I knew full well there was little room for dreaming between the pounds of flour and tattie sacks. The risk of losing my job at Johnstone's would be small, so long as my mouth stayed shut.

He barely looked up as I took my seat and let the robe fall, as I presumed was my cue —it was going to have to come off eventually. The business of selecting a pencil for his sketch was so all-consuming, he did not see how the rabbit in my chest quivered, tiny heartbeat thrumming, ready to annihilate itself at the slightest suggestion.

I gave him some tablet next, a few sittings later. It had splintered into sugary shards in the wrapper, and was thus deemed no longer fit for selling to the ladies who did their messages at Johnstone's. Broken as it was, the fudge was still gummy and sweet – the taste of summer afternoons and birthdays. This second offering amused, as much as the first had puzzled. He smiled as he massaged his moustache and said we were making good progress with the work; we'd be done by St Andrew's Day. How wonderful was that "we" to me.

He always painted barefoot. Footwear did not invite the Muse, apparently. Against the dark carpet he had down, his feet seemed almost comically flat and round, his pink toes smarting. In a strange sort of way, it made him look more awkward and naked than I was.

The Muse was no great encourager of conversation

either, for we spent hours at a stretch without saying a word. The initial discomfort that roared in my ears subsided to a bristling static, as I grew more comfortable with the fact of my body.

One afternoon, a late sun broke through the smirr and rebounded off the grey, horrid stones of the city so they glistened like rare jewels. Inside, the shadows grew warmer, though my fingertips lacked feeling from so much stillness.

I cheated my breasts just slightly to the glow, so that the warmth of sunlight yawned across them. Might they be thought of as nice breasts? Were they as good as others he'd surely seen and shaped with his brush before? I wanted him to raise his eyes and find something undeniable before him: in the shape of my hips; in the twin pools of shadow made by my collarbones; in the way I had stretched my leg out at an angle, the way those American women did in the movies. What did he think when he saw me? Was I, perhaps, simply a ragbag of limbs and features? An arrangement of shadows to take down as truthfully as possible? Did it matter that I had put every inch of myself in front of him and his canvas, though I had never shared so much of it with another man? What was it that had made him ask me to sit for him in the first place? He made no verbal appraisal, no analysis beyond a curt, "a little to the left," or, "up with the chin, a bit right with the foot". My nakedness was both an economic fact and an inspiration. This was perfectly clear to him, though less so to me.

He broke a teacup that afternoon and we finished up early.

The last time I saw him, it was a small bag of chestnuts; they were perfect specimens of the season, all dimpled and shining in brown paper. Johnstone's sold the very best ones come Christmas time. He stowed them in his satchel before we began, without disdain or comment. I rather thought he might be growing accustomed to my small offerings. He patted the soft leather flap closed with such care.

Our work was almost done; he'd apply the finishing touches in private—a little shading, some detail in the background—all of which he could complete very well without me. St Andrew's Day had come and gone. He'd been wrong about that, in the end.

I was permitted to see the thing once more, before I left. He'd made the hair even redder since I'd last looked over it. The light dappled across the skin in the palest of greens. She was familiar, the woman upon the stretched fabric, but still I could not say she was someone I recognised.

"You know, I reckon you've made me taller than I really am," I said. He smirked, as if this were some joke, and assured me he'd done no such thing. He'd put some record on his gramophone by way of celebration—something like Miller or Crosby. He swayed in time upon the spot, feet bare upon the floor, a cigarette between his long fingers.

I see him that way most often, when I think of him now.

A few years ago, I had my daughter look him up online. At the time, I gave her some excuse about his being a friend of a friend, someone I'd not thought of in fifty-odd years who just happened to pop into my head one afternoon while doing the dishes. She did not press me on it, though I doubt the explanation satisfied her.

An article on the internet says he died in France, young. A few paltry sentences strung together on a webpage that is seldom visited are all that seem to remain of him. There are no photographs, no sketches; he clearly neglected to immortalise himself along the way. All I can fix upon now is his stiff moustache, the long fingers, the bare toes. Would a self-portrait have been too out of character? He was not unsuccessful, it would seem. The online footnote they gave him implies he even sold some of his work.

My own memory is so moth-eaten, I can hardly string a line through it. I'm either standing too close or far away to decipher it. It's all pointillism, in the end.

I wonder if he knew that. He probably did, I think. He'd know it was all about composition: how things fragment and rearrange themselves; how moments make and remake themselves in oil, conspiring first against the painter, then the viewer; how grooves form in uneven brushes of dried paint, sitting atop and across one another, side by side and quite by accident. A wrist, two lips and a pelvis emerge from the nonsense.

I can no longer stand my hands. New sunspots bloom perpetually in saffron splodges and arthritic burls have transformed my fingers. The rest of it I can avoid through a combination of constant vigilance and the decision to hang no mirrors about the house, but the hands are incontrovertible. They pass before my face whenever I peel an orange or pat down my dressing gown and I cannot help it. He'd hardly want to paint me now.

My cottage hugs the crooked elbow of a quiet B-road. It's a green, nowhere sort of place near the seaside, *down south*. It's not the sort of place I might have envisioned for myself, but, every so often, the salt air tastes like smoke and iron upon my tongue and then, I might almost be watching the Clyde rush below my feet again.

The local children make a battlefield-fort of the mound of earth opposite on Sunday afternoons in the summer and I have taken to watching their little three-act dramas unfold. One has just fainted in horrible paroxysms against the lush grass; he has been struck by an arrow in the flank, now the leg, his hand across his brow as he sinks and sighs. He takes as long as he possibly may to go down; it is a marvellous little death. Another clambers up with dirt-scuffed knees to lead the charge against the neighbours to avenge him, her hair loosed against the breeze. She looks so slight she might hardly be there at all.

But the game is over all too quickly. They've caught sight

of me sitting in the kitchen window, a pale, phantom face emerging from the gloom. It's close to five and I have yet again neglected to turn a lamp on. No, not neglected – I simply decided it not worth the discomfort of lumbering to my feet to attend to the switch. I surely frighten them – the children. I frighten myself, at times. The hands are just the tip of it. They avert their eyes as they traipse past my cottage and back towards the village.

They cannot know that I might even now be in someone's hallway, or tacked against the wall of a back bathroom, or, perhaps, gathering dust against a cobwebbed attic eave. And why ever should they? It's not interesting or important in the final analysis. Besides, he left me untitled in the end. It struck me as a curious choice then, but I understand him better now. The gift was all mine and even now, I am resplendent somewhere, sunlight falling in a spearmint spray across my midriff.

Tyger! Tyger!
by Shaun Laird

Longlisted for the Edinburgh Award for Flash Fiction 2021

Get lion dung from the zoo, they said. Spread it on your flowerbeds and – Yahtzee! – no more cat problem.

So, I met with Graham the head keeper, a nervous, intense man, but happy to help.

"Any big cat should do; lions, tigers, but if I were you," he said, lowering his voice, "I wouldn't go smaller than a leopard."

One large sack of tiger scat, a bargain at £10. Or so it seemed.

Did it work? No. In fact it drew cats from far and wide – this unholy shitty catnip. They rubbed that stuff everywhere, in joyful coprophilic abandon.

The kitchen radio curtails my unhappy reverie: "… public to remain indoors. Two tigers are still on the loose; keepers at a loss to explain …"

I spy something large, striped and very, very, dangerous in my garden, watching me with yellow-eyed menace. It relieves itself on my lawn in a stream of sharp angry piss, then pads to the patio doors, its hot dank breath steaming the glass.

Two tigers …

I feel a chill wind on the nape of my neck, as I remember the living room with its open window. I turn to see the second tiger padding purposefully along the hall. Out come its claws, *click-click-clacking* on the neat Victorian tiles. Behind the creature, scarcely visible, are two neighbourhood cats, curious to see what happens next. Utter bastards.

But that's the nature of cats, I suppose. They've got each other's backs though; I'll give them that.

The night of the note I never wrote
by Karenlee Thompson

Longlisted, Scottish Arts Club Short Story Competition 2021

D*ear Dimitri,*
          I scribbled. That is his name but, in truth, I rarely call him Dimitri. I ripped the yellow page from the pad and scrunched it into a loose ball, picked it up and squeezed again, pushed it into my other palm and closed my fingers into a torturous fist around it.

He'd never liked his own name, despite loving his mother – the one who'd named him – dearly. His father had not a hand in naming him, had not loved him, and left their modest home at the earliest opportunity taking the family dog and, of all things, a broken-down rotary hoe.

Dear Dimi,

I scrawled, for that is what many of his friends call him. *This is a difficult letter to write.* Letter? Or note perhaps. A letter conjures pages – plural – perhaps by three or four. A note could be just a few words: pick up milk at shops; water plants, but not the orchid; ring the greengrocer. Or a note could be a couple of words: need bread; get fuel. Go away. Get lost. Come home. Piss off.

Dimi was the name his workmates used. Good morning Dimi, good weekend? Can I discuss these schematics with you Dimi? Nice tie, Dimi.

Architecture had always been on the cards, since high school days, since insisting on protractors and rulers in art class to fill cheap sketch pads with precise and delicate lines in pencil while the rest of us slapped primary colours about with abandon. His elevation within the firm had been swift so the casual form of address remained, albeit spoken with a certain deference of tone.

81

Dear Dee.

I wrote it but it looked silly. Only a few people called him Dee – his half-sister Sally and her friend from next door, I think. Sally's father named her, which is why she did not match her brother with a moniker like Sophia or Konstantina.

Dee. I always thought it sounded rather effeminate. My notion of him was of someone more macho, an Alpha with a soft, sensual streak.

Con's mother called him Dee Dee, leading to another high-school tag; bra cup. We were never short of nicknames.

My Darling Number Five.

One time, in our early twenties, after a huge spliff and a half packet of Tim Tams, we spoke in hushed tones about exes. He had so many, he lost count but he told me I was the best and so he named me Number One. I only had five exes – well, just brief flings really – so I thought it was hysterical to call him Number Five. That night, stoned, it was just the funniest thing. My jaw ached from laughing so much and he spat chocolate biscuit crumbs all over the television screen which made us laugh even more because the announcer looked like he was covered in rabbit shit.

I ripped the paper from the pad. Not only was Number Five not funny but, the truth was, he was no longer My Darling. Not a Darling. Not mine.

I made a pyramid of the paper balls – the discarded notes that never were – a triangle of three with the last one plonked on top.

To my Husband,

I wrote neatly on a fresh sheet. We never liked those words. Husband, wife. We did get married – in Vegas by one of those sequin-jacketed, pompadoured Elvises – but we only did it to make sure I wouldn't miss out on my grandfather's inheritance. Turreted mansion, limited edition electric blue Rolls Royce. It wasn't a difficult choice. Your Kingdom for a piece of paper. No brainer. Or so it seemed.

We survived forty years together. Seems it was no coincidence that the marriage turned acrid four months after my gnarly old grandfather finally slipped quietly out of this life.

Back in Vegas, tipsy on vodka martinis, we'd thought Grandpa – at sixty-three – was almost knock, knock, knocking on heaven's door but he hung around to squander much of his wealth and celebrate his one-hundred-and-third birthday. I inherited the lot. Which turned out to be not a lot: an antique credenza, a one-bedroom flat and a rusty Volvo that hadn't seen the highway for years.

Nixing Darling and Dear but not wanting to get too formal: *Hey Gaudi,* I wrote with that jaunty punch-in-the-arm familiarity of a friend. It was Con who first called him Gaudi when we were at Uni. Dimitri's projects had become ever more grand and protracted, with completion dates stretching out a-la Gaudi's epic *Sagrada Familia.*

Con died last summer, all shrivelled and yellow from liver cancer, so using the nickname now would probably be somewhat crass.

Off came another sheet from the lined legal pad.

Hello lover.

As I wrote it, my mind spoke it in the throaty voice I always saved for the bedroom. How ridiculous. I pressed hard and raked the pen heavily over the words, knifing through two sheets of paper. I ripped them from the pad and began tearing them into narrow strips, turning corners and trying to keep one long piece like I was peeling an apple.

I stopped using the word lover the day I discovered he had one that was not me. She was a swimming instructor at his local gym, a younger shinier model with long legs and lustrous chestnut locks that she tucked into a retro flowered bathing cap.

She didn't last too long but there were others.

A conga line of them.

To my Ex.

Scribble, rip.

To my friend.

He was once my friend. A dwindling group, especially since Con died. I spent a whole day in the hospital in those days of the dying and I know Con wanted to tell me things. The three of us had been mates since high school and Dimitri and I had watched as Con weathered an alarming number of girlfriends and wives. He'd been in and out of love his whole life but, in the end, it was me sitting there with him, not a wife or a girlfriend or a lover and not his best friend, Gaudi being too squeamish to spend more than an hour at a hospital bed.

The thing is, I knew Con wanted to tell me that I wasn't being treated right, that there were secrets and lies floating around every single day and night. I knew some of it and I didn't crave to hear any more. I especially didn't want Con to agonise over the telling so I said I knew everything and that he shouldn't worry about me in his end time.

I piled the balls of paper atop the pad and shuffled to the couch, planning a nap. How to write such a note? How could I tell this man I'd lived with for over forty years that I could not forgive him for leaving me? In the past, I forgave him for consistently cheating on me and for lying about it constantly. I forgave a string of capped swimming instructors, short-skirted secretaries, solicitors, hairdressers and all and sundry. I forgave the squandering of the – admittedly small – inheritance from my grandfather. I recently discovered he'd given my ruby ring to a now forgotten lover. Strangely, I found that forgivable.

A month or so after my grandfather died, I thought I might be the one to leave. I might finally admit that I stayed because it was comfortable, because I was lazy. I might jump back into life rather than sitting on the sidelines. I'd started staring at my naked self in the mirror. I sipped green tea outside the Viet café and eyed the men walking past, wondering if any of them would satisfy me the way Dimitri did. Despite my Number Five joke, he had always been Number One in the sack.

Could I love that one? What would this one look like first thing in the morning? A nice smile here, a pair of shiny shoes there. Here a man, there a man. Everywhere men. Men who were not Dimitri.

I convinced myself I could do it and then he walked through the doorway one afternoon, ashen, red-eyed. The father, who had left him so long ago taking the dog and the rotary hoe, was dead. I wasn't sure how it could matter so much to lose a father you barely knew but clearly the time was not right for me to leave. I listened to his vague memories. I mopped tears and made rum toddies. I loved him tenderly.

A few days later, he came home with a solicitor's letter. Not a note but a two-page missive that set out the extent of the unknown father's estate. A lush farm in the North, planted with pears and garlic, cattle roaming organically. A property I immediately pictured myself on, a lifestyle adopted in a blink. But it was barely a few beats later that I discovered I was not to be slotted in, there was no space on the farm or in his heart for me.

I did more than nap with my crumpled not-notes. I slept and dreamt. Seven hours later, the sun kissed my ear and I smiled. But my lips quivered and started a downward turn as I thought about Dimitri. He had left me then, run off to become a gentrified farmer, a process he seemed to think would be instantaneous and complete. I had cried and raged and slopped around in a fluffy dressing gown for weeks, drinking sickly port at lunchtime, eating caramel chews late at night.

Inevitably, I got dressed. Ate some vegetables. I went back to work, had drinks with girlfriends, shied away from those men I'd so recently admired.

Yesterday he sent me an email. When I saw his name there, I sat like a statue wondering what words I wanted to appear on the screen. More than anything, I think I wanted him to ask for my forgiveness, to acknowledge his monstrous character flaws. *Sorry.* That would have done.

Instead, I got a curt message – a note – asking if his mother's silver cake servers were still in the side buffet. He had forgotten about them but would like to use them for the serving of his engagement cake.

Never mind that the divorce was not yet finalized. Never mind that his mother would be on constant revolution in her grave. Never mind that Dimitri and I never had an engagement cake ourselves, let alone silver servers. Never mind.

My cheeks were wet with tears, despite the beauty and warmth of the sun. I remembered something Con said – drifting on a morphine cloud – on that last day; *always turn your face to the sunshine.*

These years later, I could hear his voice distinctly and so I turned my head and let the sun stroke me fully awake. I reached for the pad which had fallen to the tiles in the night, knowing – finally – what I should write.

It would not be a letter; he did not deserve that much effort.

It would be a short note.

Arsehole, I am . . . The doorbell rang.

Two police officers entered, both short; a rather ruddy and chubby older woman with a pudding-bowl haircut, and a slender man who looked like he should still be in school.

They came to tell me, with their sorrowful expressions and soft voices, that my husband – for that is what he still was – was dead. His leg had been mangled by some state-of-the-art tractor attachment with which he was tilling the land and he had become trapped beneath it, the blood loss causing his demise. The modern-day version of the rotary hoe, I imagined.

I made us all tea and then flipped the pad over so the officers would not see the beginning of the note I never wrote.

Nine Minutes
by Graeme McGeagh

Shortlisted for the Edinburgh Award for Flash Fiction 2021

They say when you die the soul departs the body and you're able to look down at what used to be you. I'm standing in a morgue looking down at myself; my long, blonde hair matted with blood, my complexion just off human and my fingers as cold as the stone that cracked my skull. Except, it's not me, not really, anyway.

I always said he was a maniac. Always said he was putting on a façade. I knew he had a temper and I knew he was dangerous. God knows I told enough people. But no, I was wrong, 'he's just misunderstood' claimed my sister; 'he's a nice boy,' said my mum; 'he's a top bloke' rebutted my dad. I knew better. And now here we are. I really did know better – not that it brings me one iota of comfort. As I look down at the face before me, I know I'll see it everywhere I go, every morning in the mirror, every fleeting glance in a window and every selfie to come. You said you'd always be nine minutes older than me sis, I really wish you were right. I turned on my heel knowing I'd never see her again and yet see her everywhere forevermore.

The Time-Travel Agent
by Jane Swanson

Longlisted, Scottish Arts Club Short Story Competition 2021

"Where would you like to go?' says the Time-Travel Agent.

Her eyes are dark and steady, but she avoids my gaze, and like me she wears a silver-suit with a tight-fitting hood. We are weightless, surrounded by silver 3D holograms moving like photographic ghosts that recreate the interior of a travel agency of-Old – a woman browses a glossy brochure, a cruise liner glides across a computer screen, a man in a straw hat and a teller exchange one kind of currency for another at a kiosk.

'You might like to go forwards in time to the unborn-sector,' she says.

She clicks her fingers, a hologram of a clock face appears, the pointers spin in a clockwise direction.

'Or back in time perhaps to the defunct-sector? To be honest its more popular, we have few reliable reports of what life is like in the unborn-sector.'

She clicks her fingers again, the pointers on the clock spin in an anti-clockwise direction.

'I've always been fascinated by time, the ancient Greeks had two concepts of time, *kairos,* meaning an opportune time for something to happen, and *chronos,* the chronological time, how we measure our days, our lives. Did you know for centuries people kept track of the time by studying the continuous motion of the two rotating pointers on a clock face?' I say.

'Then may I suggest an all-inclusive package holiday to eighteenth century London, which was the Golden Age of clock making,' she says.

'That is a good idea, will I travel in a time-machine?'

'Oh no it's a simple drag and drop operation now, remember how we used to drag a document and drop it into a file on a computer of-Old? It is the same sort of thing; all I need to do is drag you and drop you into someone else's life. Simple.'

'Interesting how the words 'life' and 'file' are inter-related, if you exchange the 'l' and the 'f,' the word life becomes file, is there any significance in that?'

'No idea, I am not a Deep-thinker like you,' she says.

'So, as well as visiting my destination, are you saying I will experience someone else's life?'

'Yes, that way we can give our clients an intimate and unique visitor experience.'

'Will I become that person?'

'Oh no, your hard copy stays here in the current-sector, that's the law, otherwise your actions could bring about changes to the time-space continuum, which might change the course of established events in the defunct-sector,' she says.

'Or change the course of events in the unborn-sector. Although, if events in the defunct-sector were changed, we might never notice because all subsequent events and our memories of them would alter and would therefore be consistent with the new timeline,' I say.

'Who knows! I am only a Skin-Deep Thinker, I say what I am told to say and that sort of talk makes my head spin! What will happen is this, you'll inhabit another person's body, you'll see what they see, hear what they hear and so on, but they'll be unaware that you are present,' she says.

'I see.'

'You could always opt for an upgrade to enhance your experience, that way you'll be able to access the thoughts of the person whose body you inhabit, which might be fun, but as we discussed you mustn't contribute any thoughts of your own that might change the course of established events.'

'I'll take the upgrade; will I still be able to access my Brain-Cloud of Knowledge while I am there?'

'Of course.'

'Do you have any travel tips?'

'Oh my! Be prepared for sensory overload. There's not much call for us to use our senses here, is there? Everything is sanitized, no smells, bland food, the same old holograms to look at, no objects, nothing to touch … its touch I miss the most, don't you ever wish you could feel the softness of a cat's fur, or scrunch up a dry autumn leaf in your bare hands, or feel the caress of another human beings' skin against your own?' she says.

I feel my face grow warm; why is she being so provocative, sensual talk is forbidden?

'That's brought the colour to your cheeks! I can't tell if you are angry, or embarrassed, or if it's a sign of pleasure,' she says with a glint in her eyes.

'Keep your voice down – you know that sort of loose talk is dangerous.'

She leans in close and whispers,

'I went on holiday recently to Benidorm in 1973 and my senses were on fire, I have never felt so alive! The warm sun tickled my skin, the smell of coconut suntan lotion made me feel relaxed, the sound of the crashing waves and the disco beat in the night clubs hummed in my ears, the tastes of garlic and smoked paprika tantalised my taste buds …'

She pauses, straightens her shoulders,

'And as for the colours of nature, they were almost too beautiful to behold and they deeply affected my thoughts.'

'What do you mean?'

'Surely you remember how colours affected our emotions. The sight of the blue Mediterranean Sea was calming and, at the same time it saddened me as I yearned for the world of-Old. Wild red poinsettias and trailing crimson hibiscus seeping with colour, set my heart racing, filled my head with heated thoughts of anger, bravery … and power.'

Her eyes flicker with emotion, her hand trembles as she clicks her fingers and a hologram of a well-built man appears. Silver-haired with silver rimmed spectacles, he sits hunched over a workbench with his sleeves rolled up and peers through a magnifying glass at a mass of tiny brass cogs and wheels.

'He's called William Windmill, he was a Master Clockmaker, the year is 1721,' she says.

She reaches across, touches me lightly on the shoulder and highlights my body with a glowing, yellow border.

'I've never been highlighted before! I've seen pictures from the defunct-sector of people highlighted like this, did you know they believed it was a sign that a person was Holy?' I say.

She tightens her lips; it's time for our conversation to end. She takes hold of my left shoulder and drags me towards the hologram of William. She lays my body over his image, releases her fingers and I drop into his bulky frame, a grey circle with a minus sign hovers over us both.

'How infuriating, for some reason you are not syncing,' she says.

She nips us together by the shoulders, wiggles us about and a blue circle with arrows rotating in a clockwise direction appears.

'You're syncing now, it shouldn't be long,' she says.

'Wait! Surely the arrows need to go in an anti-clockwise direction, or we will end up in the unborn-sector?'

Her eyes narrow and she forces a smile, she taps the blue circle and the direction of the arrows is reversed. William and I are synced and I experience a pleasant tingling sensation all over my body.

'Brace yourself and bon voyage!' she shouts.

Being separated from my hardcopy is like being hit sideways by a meteor. I fall into William's body with a force like that of re-entering the earth's atmosphere, my face shakes violently and my tongue is pushed into the back of my mouth. As my weightlessness decreases, I feel the first twinges of gravity in my fingers and toes. It's a soft landing; William takes most of the impact. Being of a slight build, I fit comfortably into his body. All at once I am bombarded with sensory sensations, the heft of his greasy hair upon his scalp, the bitter taste of his mouth, the furriness of his teeth, the clammy stink of his body, the roughness of his linen shirt and woollen breeches against my skin, a gnawing sensation of hunger in his stomach and the dull ache of his buttocks upon a wooden stool.

All around is a cacophony of sound – whirring drills screeching into metal, clanking hammers, ticking pendulums and chiming bells.

Thankfully, it is quiet in William's head, he is so intent on his work that he has few thoughts. I peer out of his eyes; his sight is good and I take the measure of my new surroundings. He sits at a workbench in a small first-floor room facing a large window, its cramped, four other men work at benches and the air is warmed by a wood stove in the corner of the room. William is surrounded by many kinds of small hand tools – callipers, piercing saws, steel files and pliers. Outside, the street is busy, people are dressed in ragged clothes, yet they go about their business with good cheer. I hear voices, laughter, rumbling cartwheels, horse's hooves and barking dogs.

'Have you landed?' says the Time-Travel Agent.

'Yes.'

'Comfortable?'

'Yes, its roomy and quite fascinating.'

'Good, because there is one more thing … you may be there for some time,' she says.

'What do you mean?'

'I wasn't being truthful about the unborn-sector, the reports we are receiving from that sector are grim, to prepare for what is to come, we need to delete people to save on resources.'

'Of course! Life and file! Are you saying my life is being filed away in William's body, in the same way as paper documents were filed in cabinets in the defunct-sector?'

She laughs,

'I thought you'd worked it out, maybe you're not as clever as you think you are!'

'This is outrageous! I demand to be returned at once! Why me?'

'It's not just you, all Deep-Thinkers have been selected for deletion, because you are the ones that unsettle the population with your knowledge and fancy ideas.'

'Selected by whom?'

'The New Revolutionary Committee of Skin-Deep Thinkers, lucky you spotted my mistake with the syncing, I nearly sent to the unborn-sector, trust me you are better off with William.'

'Kairos.

'What?'

'*Kairos*, that special moment when it is ripe to act, the time to take destiny into own your hands. What will become of me?'

'Be comforted, your hard copy is still here, if things improve you might return one day. But for now, all contact will cease. Good-bye,' she says.

'Wait! Come back! You can't just leave me here!'

William turns his attention to a problem with a longcase clock he's made for a wealthy client. He's discovered the steel pendulum expands and contracts with changes in temperature, which affects the timekeeping mechanism, and the clock is losing five seconds each day. He's struck by a wild thought; what if he were to make a new pendulum from a combination of different metals? That way each metal would have a differing rate of expansion and, if he got the combination right, the expansion rates in the different metals would cancel each other out and the changes in timekeeping would be negligible. If he got it right. His shoulders slump, which metals should he try, how much time will it take to get it right?

William's problem takes my mind off my own concerns and using my Brain-Cloud of Knowledge I consider the different expansion rates of metals. I've always upheld the law and never interfered with the events of the defunct-sector, but things are different now – does the law even exist? If I help William, it will change the course of established events, a solution to his problem wasn't discovered until 1726 by a clockmaker called John Harrison. If I intervene now there might never be such a thing as a Skin-Deep Thinkers Revolution. What do I have to lose? It's unlikely those retrogrades will remember me, unlikely I will ever return to the current-sector.

'William, the answer to precise time-keeping lies in making a gridiron pendulum from alternating rods of steel and brass,' I whisper.

Souvenirs
by Mary Edward

Shortlisted for the Edinburgh Award for Flash Fiction 2021

Our English grandmother raised us. We never knew our parents – only photographs. Grandmother saved us when they died and brought us from Hong Kong. Her darling babies.

Now she is dead too and as we are closing up her house, we come upon the button box. As children we were always fascinated by these treasures — cut from some amazing garments of Grandmother's exciting past and clothes which belonged to our parents. Each of them had a story, from the jewelled buttons of Grandfather's smoking jacket or Dad's pilot uniform to the little satin buttons of our mother's wedding dress. We were enchanted, Melanie and I. Grandmother would sit with us, the buttons scattered on the kitchen table and tell us magical tales of the events these buttons had once known.

'What delightful souvenirs!' Melanie says now, as we pour the buttons out.

Then we see, folded on the bottom of the box and quite yellowed by time, a small newspaper cutting. From The South China Times, dated 3rd July 1997.

I unfold it as Melanie looks on.

Couple Take Twins to England

The new-born girl twins, found abandoned in an alleyway downtown a month ago, have joined the British exodus as the Union Jack is lowered in Hong Kong for the last time. Diplomat Marcus St John Wells and his wife, who are childless, leave today with the famous babies to be brought up in England.

My sister and I turn to each other. We have no words.

The Eye of Horace
by Gail Anderson

Longlisted, Scottish Arts Club Short Story Competition 2021

He was not the only man to be laid low by an unrelenting schedule, undone by obsession. Horace knew, in fact, that his travails placed him shoulder to shoulder with his hero, archaeologist Howard Carter, discoverer of Tutankhamun's tomb. Carter had roamed a desert, searched fruitlessly, lost all faith and credibility – before finally attaining his dream.

As had Horace.

There were differences of scale, of course. Horace's unrelenting schedule was the timetable of the S14 bus – a meandering route between his own tidy village and the big city to the south where, to his joy, he was offered a job as docent in the Antiquities Wing of a world-famous museum. On that first fateful morning, Horace left his house with a glad heart, his soft frame clad in his smartest suit. He walked to his stop, boarded the 07.17 bus – and laid eyes on the driver.

Amanda.

It wasn't her golden coiffure, wound and piled atop her head like Pharaoh's cobra, that drew his gaze; nor the queenly bosom that strained the buttons of her sky-blue uniform. It was her eyes. Amanda was fantastically farsighted, and the spectacles she donned to work her ticket machine magnified her green irises to the size of Moghul Emeralds. Horace, a bachelor, felt his heart plucked cleanly away, a reliquary in the hands of a looter.

'City centre, please,' he stammered.

'Single?' asked Amanda.

'Oh yes,' he sighed.

This discussion was resumed the following morning.

'Return to city centre, please.'

'Oh, not single after all?'

Amanda's eyelashes fluttered like tiger butterflies against hothouse glass. Horace, patting his overheated brow with his ticket, made his way to a seat and considered the challenge before him.

How was he to woo a woman he could speak with for only ten seconds at a time? There were always people queueing behind him. The front seat nearest the driver was occupied by a banker-type in a pinstripe suit. The man had the look of a regular commuter – black satchel at his side, newspaper open in front of his face. Horace scowled at the banality of the headlines. *Dog fouling... council minutes... a spate of local burglaries.* Clearly, Horace's best chance of speaking with Amanda was to board the bus before the banker and secure the front seat. But how?

When Howard Carter set about finding Tutankhamun's tomb, he developed a system. He mapped the Valley of the Kings into a series of grid-blocks; then he and his team worked through each block systematically – clearing the ground, trowelling, uncovering – before moving to the next. This tedious process occupied many years before yielding results.

Horace consulted his S14 timetable, and the following Monday he left the house early to board Amanda's bus one stop prior to his own. He boarded at successively earlier stops along the route each day for the next two weeks, hoping to beat the banker to the front seat. Finally, he reached the stop at the edge of his village, where hedgerows and green fields stretched to horizon.

The bus arrived. The banker was still *in situ*.

Horace told his troubles to Andy at the monthly meeting of the Megaliths and Recumbents Society.

'Sounds a hopeless case, mate,' Andy said, not what Horace wanted to hear. 'Why not take Aileen out for a drink after the meeting? Nice woman. Fancies you.'

Aileen was undoubtedly a nice woman. She had insightful things to say about Mesopotamian vessel shards and dendrochronology. They'd hit it off at more than one Society meeting, finding common ground on Jurassic lime and field methods. Moreover, Aileen had been to Egypt. Horace reflected; then pulled himself up short.

Carter hadn't wavered. Even as others had declared the Valley of the Kings exhausted, Carter and his team persevered, moving 70,000 tons of sand and gravel, an effort mocked by the world as a hopeless pursuit.

'I've got to see this thing through,' he said, narrowing his eyes.

Horace bought a bicycle. He rose early, pedalled beyond the village to a new and more distant bus stop each day. On lonely verges he stood amid candy wrappers and sheep. He plumbed hamlets and forgotten market crosses. His tyres carved rifts through yellow leaves as autumn melted into winter and the mornings darkened, week on week. After thirty-eight days, the banker's bus stop remained a mystery. Still, Horace was seeing rewards.

His soft physique was gaining definition – so much so that he was forced to purchase new clothes. Black jeans and polo necks hid the road moisture and gave him an uncharacteristically trendy look. He purchased a black messenger's bag to carry fresh clothes, ready for a quick shower and change in the museum's staff facilities.

Best of all, Amanda began to notice him.

'You must be a spy with a girl in every village,' she quipped, morning forty-three.

'Two steps ahead of the Russians,' he replied, raising a jaunty eyebrow.

'And one step ahead of a jealous husband?'

Horace was sure he saw hunger in her enormous eyes.

'Single to Nether Crudwell,' boomed the farm woman

behind him, nudging Horace in the leg with her brolly.

Others noticed him too. At the museum, Alice from Etruscan Pottery brought him little gifts of pastry, while Enid from China to 800 AD provided fresh cream for his staff-room coffees. And there was Aileen at the Megaliths and Recumbents.

'That job in the city suits you,' she said. 'You're looking sharp.'

'And you,' he said. 'Lovely necklace.'

She wore a cloisonné Egyptian eye, symbol of his near namesake.

'Horus,' she said, 'the half-blind.'

According to myth, the falcon god's left eye had been gouged out by Set, god of disorder and chaos.

Horace, uncomfortable, shuffled his feet. 'But he did regain his sight.'

'He did,' she said, frowning. 'Finally.'

Horace's new lifestyle had its dark side. He was short on sleep, long on road miles. Most importantly, he still hadn't managed to board the bus ahead of the banker. Day in, day out, the man occupied the front seat, satchel at his side, paper in front of his odious face. Even the headlines were unchanged: a long-running spate of burglaries that had police baffled. Horace cursed the man's unfailing good health.

Then – morning seventy-seven – Horace's luck changed.

He'd ridden forty-six minutes through the dark to Hepworth's Halt, an old coaching inn on a lonely crossroads. There, standing alone at the bus stop, display handkerchief glowing by the light of a full moon, stood the banker. Horace joined him, a queue of two in a silvery darkness. The banker turned to him with hooded eyes.

'His ghost still walks those halls, you know.' An Etonian voice, offhand.

100

Horace felt a chill. 'Who's ghost?'

The banker's gaze never left Horace's face. He raised a finger towards the inn.

'Claude the Highwayman.'

'Why are you telling me this?'

The man held up his newspaper, clutched in a slender, gloved hand. *Cat Burglar Strikes Again.* Horace took an involuntary step back.

'It's no wonder the police are baffled,' the banker whispered, 'If their quarry is a ghost.'

He laughed softly. Horace felt the back of his neck tingle. Then the bus arrived, headlights cutting the night, and Horace's heart surged. He'd finally discovered the banker's stop. Tomorrow the coveted front seat would be his.

Day seventy-eight fell auspiciously on the exact day, all those years ago, that Carter had discovered the Boy King's tomb. *The day of days,* Carter would later write, *the most wonderful I have ever lived through.* Lathered with nerves, Horace cycled north that morning with the wind at his back to the bus stop beyond Hepworth's Halt. Today he would have the pleasure of speaking with Amanda properly for the first time.

But it was not to be. The front seat was taken. Not by the banker – oh no, it was worse than that. The seat was filled by a strapping, dark-haired, devil-may-care type.

'If I were that cat burglar, baby,' the man was saying to Amanda as Horace boarded, 'there'd be just one thing at your house I'd take.'

'You'd be welcome to it.' Amanda shot a look of smouldering lust towards this country villain.

As the bus got underway, the man slid panther-like from his seat and leaned against the driver's enclosure. Horace watched for five hellish minutes until they arrived at Hepworth's. There the man bestowed one final look of filthy intent on the now clearly gagging-for-it Amanda. Then he swaggered off the bus, turned and looked back at her, arms folded. The banker was nowhere to be seen. Horace stumbled to the front seat.

'Who was that?' he blurted, guard dropped.

'Night foreman at Bird's Custard,' she said, blowing a kiss out the door. 'My husband.'

The lightning bolt that pierced Horace's heart was thrown by Set himself. Even as his blood turned to resin, Horace's lips, functioning independently, spoke the opening line he'd been rehearsing for weeks.

'Do you know, a hoard of Roman coins was found not far from here....'

'Oh, really?' Amanda's eyes flicked to the wing mirror. Her arm was out the window, waving.

Then two burly policemen stepped aboard and took Horace away.

Brilliant Buswoman Bags Burglar screamed the tabloid headlines the following morning. The evidence against him was watertight. Horace's trial was a mere formality.

'How would you describe the behaviour of the accused during the months he rode your bus?'

'I knew right away he was up to no good, that one,' said Amanda, popping her gum, pyrite hair glinting beneath the courtroom's pendant lights.

'Never got on at the same stop. Always dressed in black. Always carried that bag, God-knows-what inside it. Told me himself he was one step ahead of the law.'

Detectives brandished incident maps correlating Horace's bus-boarding pattern with the burglaries. His bicycle, ID'd by half the ridership of the S14, was wheeled into court as evidence – and along with it, a black satchel loaded with silver candlesticks, which police had found draped across the handlebars.

Horace recognised the bag at once. It belonged to the

banker.

Testifying in his own defence, Horace admitted to his hideous infatuation, his erratic behaviour. As for the burglaries – it was the banker they wanted! But no one seemed to remember the man in the front seat of the bus, the one with a newspaper held up in front of his face. Horace's defence didn't sound convincing, even to himself. As testimony ended, he raised hopeless eyes to the heavens and saw a sight that struck him like a chisel: Aileen – faithful Aileen – tight-lipped in the gallery. As they led him away, the tickertape in Horace's brain displayed the words carved on Howard Carter's lonely tomb. *O night, spread thy wings over me as the imperishable stars.*

Horace had always rejected the 'curse of the Pharaohs' as tabloid frenzy. Now he wasn't so sure. When a letter arrived from Aileen in the first week of his incarceration, Horace couldn't bear to open it. For the time being, he dwelt in *Duat*, the underworld, attended by jackals and his spirit endured Osiris's fabled 'weighing of the heart'. Heavy hearts, he knew, tipped and fell into the jaws of demons. Horace kept Aileen's sealed letter in his breast pocket and hoped for balance.

When Carter first opened Tutankhamun's tomb, he couldn't see clearly for the darkness and dust that clouded his vision. Now, blinking in bright daylight at the end of his term, Horace slid his thumb under the gummed flap of the letter. Read the words written inside. Heard his hero's voice crackle through the ether. *Gold, everywhere, the glint of gold...* Horace wiped tears from his eyes and saw, waiting for him just outside the gates, treasure beyond all imagining.

Empty
by Torya Winters

Shortlisted for the Edinburgh Award for Flash Fiction 2021

The beetroot bruises under her skin reveal the violence of their attempts to save her. Her hand lies in mine, floppy and translucent like a dead jellyfish. I watch as her chest is forced up and out, over and over again, by the harsh plastic tubing down her throat.

This is not what I had imagined when that embryo implanted. I saw a future where we planted wildflowers together, where I placed my hands over hers and taught her the intricacies of knitting and crochet. Now those same hands shield one so small that a single finger dwarfs her entire leg.

Bitter tears sting and blur my eyes. My fucking womb couldn't do the one thing it was meant to do. I took the vitamins, injected myself with the hormones, all it had to do was provide the safe haven.

Another woman left yesterday, baby attached to oxygen tank, car seat brandished by her partner like a trophy. Belle lies still in her plastic tank, limbs cradled by a rolled-up towel, forever denied the chance to graduate.

I watch numbly as each lifesaving line slides out and her tiny eyelids flutter closed. I snip a strand of the soft down from her head and press her inky feet against a card to remember their shape. One last kiss on her forehead and that's it.

I leave with my paperwork, the bald facts. Extreme prematurity.

Abruption.

Hysterectomy.

I am hollow, just the scent of her sweet breath in my memories.

Egg Summer
by Lucy Grace

Longlisted, Scottish Arts Club Short Story Competition 2021

Lenny Beckworth said he had a skylark's, but nobody believed him. He said a lot of things. He said his brother was in the army, but we knew he was in Borstal – my mam saw his mam getting on the bus early in the morning and she wasn't back in time for work. You can't visit people if they're in the army, they don't let you, and anyway the bus doesn't go there and you might get shot by a bullet.

But Lenny couldn't help it.

"And I've got an owl's," he said.

"You've never got an owl's. What kind of owl then?" demanded Jack Nickson. Jack Nickson was supposed to have the best collection all round and even he didn't have an owl's.

"It's a barn owl."

"What colour is it then?"

"It's … brown."

Jack knew he had him.

"With specks on?"

"Er, yeah. Brown, with specks."

"Are they black specks or white specks?" Jack was relentless. The rest of us watched him, not sure where this was going. I did, though. I knew the egg of a barn owl was white and smooth and surprisingly small. I knew this because I had three at home, curled in sheep's wool. But I didn't tell.

"It's hard to say – the specks are black and brown, I think." Lenny was sounding less confident now, but Jack had moved closer towards him.

"So, let me get this right, at home you have a brown barn owl's egg, with black and brown specks on it. And is it big?"

105

Lenny thought about the size of an owl in flight and hedged his bets.

"Of course it is," he said. "Owls are massive."

Jack Nickson folded his arms. The other boys started walking away across the field with the football. I stood on the bottom bar of the fence, looking away across the grass. Jack had hold of Lenny like a mouse and was squeezing him to death. I thought of his thin face and runny nose and dirty fingernails and it made my stomach hurt.

Jack Nickson leaned right in towards Lenny's closed mouth.

"Your barn owl egg is about as real as your army brother," he said quietly and fiercely. "It's bullshit."

Lenny didn't move, he just stood there looking past Jack's left ear into the sky, waiting. But Jack had finished. The fence bar bounced as he climbed on it, over to the pitch.

After the game we lay down on our backs under the blue sky, run out. From high above came the liquid song of the skylark. Jack snorted.

"A bloody brown owl's egg and a skylark's – yeah right, Lenny Beckworth, yeah right." And I looked up into the blue and thought about hitting Jack Nickson hard in the mouth.

"Seen any owls recently, Lenny-boy?"

I was walking home after school. Behind me I heard slowing feet and I swallowed. Jack Nickson peeled himself from the warm bricks of the wall and stood across the path.

"Show me, then. Show me your owl and your skylark."

There was a piece of blue string in the gutter, I wanted to pick it up.

"Well, I haven't got them now, have I, I haven't brought 'em to school." Lenny was unconvincing.

"Go an' get 'em an' I'll see you at the end of your ginnel. Five o'clock."

Jack walked away without looking at me and Lenny's shoulders slumped. I spoke to him, quickly.

"What're you going to do?"

"I'm going to have to show him, aren't I?"

"But have you got them?"

"I said I did, didn't I?"

Lenny met my eyes then and I saw a feral cat, wanting.

"Will you be there at five, just in case?" he asked.

"Just in case what?"

But we both knew what he meant. Jack Nickson loved performing to a crowd.

"Just in case. You know where I live, don't you?"

Everybody knew where Lenny Beckworth lived. Since his dad was killed in Underwood pit and his brother was taken to Borstal, they'd moved to the flat above the Co-op down on Wharf Road. They only had two rooms and a bit of a kitchen, all right for a single man, said my mam, but not a family, even if it only had two people in it. My mam had seen his mam get turned away in the shop when she wanted a loaf on tick, Mr Marriot had said her tick was too long already. My Dad was dead an' all but we still lived in a house.

I didn't say yes or no, just nodded once as I walked off. I went the long way back.

At home my mam was at the washing line and I pinched a slice of bread from the table before running upstairs. She shouted after me.

"Don't you go disappearing again lad – it's tea in ten minutes if you want feeding."

Under the bed was my egg collection. It was an old cutlery box, little compartments separated by pieces of wood. Each contained an egg or two, along with a little label with a date on the back. I'd made little nests for them out of sheep's wool I'd pulled from the fences and the eggs cosied warmly together, safe. I lifted out one of the owl's and one of the skylark's eggs, putting them carefully in the bit of sock and the sock in the toffee tin and the tin in my pocket. After sliding the collection away again I clattered down the stairs and out the door before my mam knew which brother I was.

The church clock hadn't chimed quarter to when I got to Lenny's, but he was already sitting on the kerb outside the Co-op. I sat down next to him and the tin stuck into my leg.

"All right?" I asked.

"No," replied Lenny. I looked at the side of his face as he threw stones across the road. I felt the stomach ache again and before I knew what I was doing I passed him the tin.

"Here."

Lenny held it with both hands.

"Go on, open it. It's to show Jack Nickson."

Lenny opened the tin and looked at the bit of sock.

"Inside."

Carefully, Lenny put his fingers inside and lifted out the first egg, white and smooth. He looked at me.

"Barn owl," I said. "They're not brown."

Lenny gently lifted the second egg and looked at me again.

"Skylark?" he asked. But before I could answer there was the scrawk of brakes up the road and Jack Nickson was riding down on his bike, a few younger kids with him. Quick as a flash Lenny put the eggs and the tin in his pocket and stood up.

"Here you are then," said Jack Nickson, throwing his bike to the ground. "Show me your eggs."

I waited for Lenny to get the tin out.

"What eggs?" said Lenny.

I felt sick.

"Barn owl's? Skylark's? Remember anything, stupid?"

Lenny's hand covered his shorts pocket.

"I don't have any eggs," said Lenny. "It were a lie."

Jack Nickson was on him in a second. He caught Lenny by surprise with the first punch and knocked him to the ground. The others crowded around the scuffle and there

108

was a metal clink as the tin fell out of his pocket. The lid had come off and the sock lay limply on the ground like a grass snake after a mouse dinner. Jack let go of Lenny and moved towards it.

Immediately I stepped forward and stamped hard on the piece of sock. There was a crunch. Jack pushed me backwards and bent down. Tiny bits of broken eggshell were stuck in the wool.

"What's this?" he asked.

One of the others shouted, "Hit him an' all, Jack."

I spoke quickly. "It was for you, Jack. It's mine, I brought it for you, a skylark's."

Jack Nickson stared at me. Lenny was holding his face, testing his bottom lip for blood, his nose running with snot. He looked away down the street.

"Pity it broke, then," said Jack. "Get me another."

"Course," I said. "I've got another."

The bang of a ginnel gate made us look round. Lenny was gone.

"Tomorrow," Jack Nickson said to me, picking up his bike. The others let him through and they all went away down the street.

I walked halfway home, late for tea, before turning and running back down to the Co-op. I went down the ginnel and stood in the yard at the back.

"Lenny?" I shouted. "Lenny, it's me."

Lenny looked out. His lip was swollen and his right eye was turning purple on his sallow skin.

"You coming or what?" I called.

We walked back up to my house.

"Do you want to come in?"

Before he'd replied my mam came out into the yard.

"There you are. And Leonard too – how lovely to see you, Leonard. It's tea time, go and get washed, I'll get you something."

I said nothing. This was different, mam was different. She didn't say anything about me being late, about Lenny's bashed up face or dirty nails.

I made Lenny take his shoes off at the bottom of the stairs and his heel stuck out through his sock like a bone. In my room, I pulled out the cutlery box with the glass lid and Lenny's eyes nearly fell out of his head. He put his dirty nails on the glass and stroked the eggs in their nests.

"Wow," he said quietly.

I read the little cards to him. He sat on the floor and listened, smoothing his swollen lip with his thumb and listening. I felt a bit funny again.

"Here," I said. "You should start a collection."

I tipped out the sheep's wool biscuit tin and pushed it towards him.

"You can have this. Make a little nest with the wool, look."

I showed him how to pull at the softness until it made a little circle with a dent inside.

"I don't have any eggs," said Lenny, for the second time that day. If anyone else had said it I would have said they were asking, but not Lenny. I knew he never asked for anything. I passed him two swaps: a tiny robin's egg, creamy and speckled, and a song thrush's egg, slightly bigger and a deep blue.

"Each egg needs its own nest," I said. "You'd better make a few more, ready."

We worked together in silence for another few minutes until mam shouted up.

"Tea's out!"

When he reached for his third slice of bread my Mam didn't say nowt but I noticed that his fingernails were clean and short. The clippers were back on the mantlepiece next to the clock and dad's last army photo. We had extra pudding.

110

"What are you doing after school tomorrow, Leonard?"

My mam was standing at the sink, she didn't see Lenny duck his head.

"Er, nothing, Mrs Shaw. Just going home for tea an' that."

"Doesn't your mother work evenings?"

"She leaves me a sandwich."

Lenny didn't mention breakfast. Mam was drying the blue plate, going round and round on the same bit. I stopped chewing.

"We have tea at five, usually. Same every day. And you can always sleep here, on our Robert's floor, if she's out."

Lenny was blinking and nodding, biting his injured lip. His eyes were watering.

"You've had a rough time of it lately, what with your brother leaving and your father gone. It's hard for your mother. You're welcome here."

I had a lump in my throat but it wasn't bread. My mam was brilliant and I loved her.

After tea we went out in the yard until Lenny said he had to go home.

"I'll see you tomorrow," he said.

I nodded, but it might have been too dark for him to see.

"See you tomorrow," I said. "We can do more eggs. I've got another skylark's."

At the pass of the bodies
by Paul Bristow

Longlisted, Scottish Arts Club Short Story Competition 2021

Bealach nan Corp winds around Ben Ledi and over to St Bride's church. Like all coffin roads, it's not an easy road. It isn't supposed to be. Its twists and turns are meant to confuse, to disorientate. Not the mourners you understand, but the spirits of those in the carried coffins. It wouldn't do to have a poor soul decide to find its way back home. And of course, there are other sorts of spirits to be found on roads such as these. Or so I'm told.

I think it would take more than spirits to startle me these days. Would need to be noisy spirits too, I'm deaf in one ear now and the other just rings all the time. Silence. That's what would startle me. A moment of quiet. Even here, up amongst the hills around Callander, the bells ring always in my ear, echoing around my head.

The air is certainly better though, away from the smoke and rubble of the towns. Even though it's over, the war is still everywhere to be seen. It will be for years yet. I was glad of a reason to leave. I haven't settled since we got back. Even after a year. With our home in Bethnal Green gone, there was no bed I could sleep in. No company I could keep. Always just the memories and the bells.

I had a friend in the military, Atkins, who took pity on me more than anything. He said he'd found me a mission, something that could use my talents. As if we were back surveying in Belgium. "Next war will be different," he said, just like that, as if we all hadn't just spent six years dying. "Top brass think we'll need rocket launch pads in places off the beaten track. Out in the hills and countryside. Need you to do some scoping out for us up in Scotland. Well paid, your pick of the best bed and breakfasts. And all the fresh air and exercise you could need. You can … start to put all this behind you. Maybe even start again."

Start again? It seemed inconceivable. I was stuck and felt sure I would stay stuck until after the enquiry, until the truth of the disaster was made plain. If ever it would be. It wasn't Atkins place to comment on such matters, he couldn't even if he wanted to. It was a kind offer though and so I took it in the spirit in which it was intended. To be honest, I'm still not sure he didn't just send me off politely on a wild goose chase to keep me out of the way. Still, I take my measurements and photos, mark off the maps and post them down at the end of each week. It's up to the men in suits what happens next. Though it would be a shame to spoil the hills with bombs and rockets. Surely no good can come of that. No good at all.

I sometimes wonder that we take our relationship with the land for granted – cutting, ripping, digging. It's in places such as these that the land cuts back, is more ready to defend itself. Or to simply just exist in its own raw glory, without concern or regard for us. The corpse roads respect the landscape, clinging to the edges of bogs and winding through empty valleys, criss-crossing rivers. To call them roads though is to diminish them. These are not roads, they are ways. Ways of getting from one place to another, a narrow thread weaving between well tilled fields that coffins must not cross and hills higher than mourners can clamber. Surveying, you come to recognise the feel of these places in between. Or at least, I do. Stairwells on the underground, randomly untouched houses in streets bombed to rubble, or the edge of the countryside where trees give way to streets and houses. And older places, where you may find way-markers and boundary stones to help draw invisible lines across the land. Since the war I've found a similar sensation to be found in those sleepless hours, when the rest of the world lies silent, and I sit open eyed in the dark, the endless bells chiming in the dawn.

And this is how I felt when I first walked through Bealach

nan Corp. But there was something else, around those frayed edges, that called to some primal part of me to be ready, be aware. A feeling I remembered from the days of running for cover. I reasoned at first that this was because I was alone with dusk approaching. But I quickly realised that I was uneasy precisely because I did not feel alone.

The ground was hard with frost and so I could clearly hear the crunch of boots on the ground. No matter which direction I turned to, there was no one to be seen. But still the boots crunched. Of course, I knew that hills and valleys could distort sounds, making things seem nearer than they actually were, so I called out a greeting to whoever was nearby. There was no reply. Or at least, no reply from another voice, for instead there was a crack and a splash.

I turned towards a nearby loch I had noted on the right of the path, fearing I might see my mysterious fellow traveller struggling in the icy water. The loch was still and frozen. Beyond it though, at the top of the hill, there was a light. It seems strange to report, but somehow, the presence of that light in the empty valley, somehow made the day seem darker, as if rather than illuminating the darkness, it was drawing attention to it. The light swayed and shifted and I could not yet make out who held it. There were voices now too, as if at a great distance, calling out, screaming.

And then, a voice I recognised too well, singing, singing in time with the bells.

"It's a lovely day tomorrow, tomorrow is a lovely day."

I knew what this was, had felt this before as butterflies turned to bats in my chest. I'm not ashamed to say I ran down from the hill and made swiftly to the inn where I was staying, trying to outstep the darkness, moving as quickly as I could until the voices were gone and only the familiar ringing remained.

I have learned these last years, that it is better to talk about what you fear, to give it form and shape that you can understand. From many years surveying, I also know the best way to solve a mystery is usually to speak to a local. So, I shared my experience with the innkeeper that night after dinner.

"Small wonder," he said, "there's probably as many people died up on that road as were ever carried along it in coffins."

"Really? How so?"

"There was an accident, eighteen fifties or thereabouts. Funeral party got lost on the way to Saint Bride's. Well over a hundred of them, all walking the coffin road in midwinter. It wasn't dark when they set out, but they had torches with them all the same, all these lights weaving slowly round the hills. It had been a cold few days, but as they're at the pass, the snow started. You've seen what it's like up there, it's easy enough to lose your way when you can see where you're going. Whoever was at the head of the funeral party took a wrong turn and led them all out across the frozen loch. It took a moment or two for them to notice, then they heard the first crack of the ice. Everyone panicked, scrambled and ran, and of course the ice shattered all the quicker, taking them right down into the depths."

"The loch up there? I stood across from it today, it's surely never big enough for over a hundred people to fall into."

"Deeper than it looks. They never recovered all the bodies though. The snow had come in fierce and didn't clear for days. Took about that long for people to realise the funeral party had never made it through the pass. In between times, the lake had frozen back over. Some of the poor souls had floated back up to the top and there were all these dead hands reaching up out of the ice when it froze again. The animals had been chewing at them. Drowned faces too, peering up at you from below. They had to take picks and hammers to the ice to smash through and drag

115

them up, even then there was only so much they could do – the loch didn't thaw properly till the spring. They never found so much as a splinter of the coffin."

"That's dreadful," I said. "You think I was hearing spirits then?"

"You'll know better than I what you heard. But people do say they hear the cries for help echoing across the loch. We've had a few folk since then just wander off the path and end up dead in the loch themselves. Some will tell you that's because they saw the lights of the funeral party and felt compelled to follow them through the pass straight down into the loch and onto the hereafter."

"There were lights on the hill tonight …"

"There's been lights flickering all around these hills and fields since long before a funeral party disappeared."

I nodded, I had certainly read plenty about this phenomenon before, "Will-o'-the-wisps and magic lanterns. It could well be these are just part of the natural order of things in a way we don't yet understand."

"Could be. But that's not what I meant. I've heard lots of stories like yours and I've come around to thinking that it's not just the spirits of those on the coffin road up there. Places like that … they pull spirits towards them. Or there's those who have loved ones that are just following them about. And when they're there, they get lost on the winding paths. I'd say half the ghosts up there are those that people brought with them. If you're surveying again tomorrow, I'd make sure you're done before dark."

I took him at his word. So, here I am, back at the pass, waiting for darkness. Only this time, I know what to expect.

Snow has started to fall, thick and fast. My breath freezes on the air, my fingers are numb and just as I think I might give up, I hear the cracking of boots on the frost. This time, I see them more clearly, grey shapes through the blizzard, walking out across the ice. It begins, the screaming, the cries for help. I turn away.

There are others too now, passing by me on the road, lost in the snow, wandering the coffin road trying to find a way home. And finally, I see her, as I knew I would. She smiles just as she did in the days before the war. Before I left her to the raids and the chaos. I hear the crying and screaming again and it may be the funeral party out upon the ice, or the women and children trampled and dying on the bomb shelter stairway. It almost does not matter. She carries a torch to light my way safely and I follow her. My boots crunch on the frozen ground as I step from the land onto the loch.

The bells stop ringing.

Instead, there is only her voice, singing the song from the day I marched away.

"If today your heart is weary,

If ev'ry little thing looks grey,

Just forget your troubles and learn to say,

Tomorrow is a lovely day."

She stops. Finally, there is quiet, no screaming, no singing, no bells.

Her cold hand reaches out for me and she draws me slowly into that silence.

One Small Step
by Brendan Thomas

Shortlisted for the Edinburgh Award for Flash Fiction 2021

Apollo 11 moved into position on the launch pad. The team gathered for the last time in a windowless meeting room filled with cigarette smoke, stale sweat and the remnants of a catered lunch.

"Any last-minute decisions before we conclude?" the team leader asked, eyeing his watch.

An engineer said, "Have we decided on the first man to step out?"

"The Lunar Module Pilot is always first to exit," the leader answered. "That's Buzz."

"But the exit hatch is on the opposite side of the module next to Neil."

"Buzz can climb across Neil."

"The backpacks on the suits are too bulky. Buzz's suit damaged the Lunar Module mock-up yesterday when we tried that manoeuvre. We can't risk damaging the real Module on the moon's surface," the Engineer answered.

The leader ran his fingers through his tired hair before speaking,

"So Neil goes first, then Buzz."

"Exactly."

"Is that a problem for anyone?" he asked, eyeing each of the three astronauts.

Buzz Aldrin was first to speak, "History will remember the team that conquered the moon, not just the first person to walk on its surface," he said.

Command module pilot Michael Collins agreed. "Neil goes first, then Buzz. Anything else?"

"Should I prepare a little speech for my exit, man's first words from the moon's surface?" Neil asked.

The leader dismissed him with a wave. "Everyone will be enthralled with the pictures beamed into their homes. No one will remember what you say."

Anne
by Alan Howley

Longlisted, Scottish Arts Club Short Story Competition 2021

The Guards are here. In the front room. Filling it up. She is sitting on the two-seater. Looking at them. Trying to listen to them. The window is at her back. Small pieces of dust are moving in the light. She wonders where her husband is. She wonders what can be taking him so long. The television guide is in front of her. She moves it. Lining it up with the corner of the table.

They rang the doorbell. A small amount of time ago. Two of them. An older one. He is about forty. He has hair that needs a trim. And a girl one. She looks twenty-five. The youngest grandchild is twenty-five. Or twenty-six. She is a hairdresser inside in town. This one is a Guard. She looks nice. She has a smile at the side of her eyes. This is a lovely room, Mrs Lynch. She speaks a bit loud. Like there is traffic. Or the Hoover is going.

It is Tuesday. In the morning time. Definitely Tuesday. She wonders where her husband is. She wonders what can be taking him so long. The shops are only ten minutes away. When they rang the doorbell, she thought it must be him. That he'd left his keys. It wasn't him. It was these two. These two Guards.

Is he dead? she had said.

Excuse me?

My husband. Sean, is he dead?

We're not here about your husband.

Oh, she had said. Then a moment later; oh, again.

Do you mind if we come in?

She had stood aside. Let them pass her. They seemed wide in her hallway. And now she is here. On her own. In the front room. And they are here. Two Guards. One is standing. He has his arms folded. He has his legs wide apart. He is not looking at her. He is looking at the room. At things. And one is sitting. The girl one. She is perched on the edge of the cushion. In Sean's chair. Daddy's chair. Her knees touch each other. Her shoes are the kind a man on a building site wears. She is talking. It is tiring to listen. She is talking about the old house. Caherconlish. Why are they asking about the old house?

Sure, we haven't been there in years, she says.

How long, would you think?

After Gerard left for college, she says.

He went to Germany, she says.

To study, she says.

The other two were older. They had gone already. The house was empty. They didn't need all the space. It was getting hard to keep it clean. Costing too much to keep it warm. They were getting old. There was nothing new to say. And none of those children were ever going to be back.

Sean wanted to move to the sea, she says.

So we did, she says.

The man shifts. The floorboard under him makes a noise. He looks at her. He is holding a photograph. He has taken it from the shelf over the fire. It is of Sean. A long time ago. He has hair. The frame is silver. It has two dents. It is tarnished at the bottom left corner. It is a holiday photograph. It is Spain. Playa Blanca. Very fancy. Most people went to Kerry. This was just after the baby. Just after Jude. Sean is in a deck chair. The material is striped. He has one arm above his head. To cool himself down. His sunhat is white. He has swimming trunks on. They are green. They have purple swirls. They look a bit too small for him. It is a bright day. Everything is covered in whiteness. The image is faded. Sean is protesting his picture being taken. He is smiling too. Like everything was OK. Like nothing had happened. Like they weren't here to forget. We can have another, Annie.

121

Mrs Lynch, the young one says, the people in Caherconlish called us.

Caherconlish?

Yes, where you used to live.

Not for years though, she says.

Yes. No, we know that. You said. But the people who live there now? Well, they contacted us. Contacted the Guards.

Oh, she says.

Oh indeed, says the man.

It is the first time he speaks. He doesn't use words right, she thinks. He makes them mean other things, she thinks. And his voice sounds wrong. Doesn't fit his face. Doesn't match the size of him, his bulk. He is still holding the picture. He breathes on the frame. At the tarnished corner. He rubs it with his sleeve. He examines where he has rubbed. Out damn spot, he says, to the frame. He smiles at her. Now he is being funny, she thinks. He puts the photograph back on the shelf. The stain is still there.

Yes, he says. They discovered something. In the back garden.

He looks at her. She looks at him. She doesn't blink. She looks down. At his shoes. She looks at her own shoes. The back garden. They discovered something, she hears him say. Inside her on the ocean floor a sleeping thing stirs. It has not been awake for a long, long time. She feels it in her tummy. This creature, moving. It gathers itself and shakes the sand and detritus and layers of dead off itself. The water becomes cloudy. She is frightened. I thought you were gone, she thinks. The sadness had been a never-ending night.

Building a new house at the end of the garden they were, he says. Digging down for to lay foundations they were. When they happened across it. A small little, what was the word they used, Tara?

Bundle.

That was it. Bundle. A small bundle. Wrapped in what

122

had been a blanket, or towel maybe.

She moves her head. To stop looking at him. She looks at the television guide. On the cover is the man who does that quiz. He is smiling. She looks at his hair. She doesn't blink. Her vision blurs a little. A film of liquid forms on her right eye. It gathers on the bottom lid. Teetering.

Jude, she says. That will be Jude.

Excuse me? says Tara.

In the hole, she says.

In the garden, she says.

In the blanket, she says. Blue, it was. Powder blue, she thinks. For a boy.

Mrs Lynch, the girl says. What are you saying to us?

The girl's lips are moving. And there is sound coming out. She is saying words. And more words. She hears it. Anne. Anne hears it. My name is Anne, she thinks. I can hear the sounds this wee girl is making. Inside my front room. Now. Today. I wonder what she is saying. Her noise is woolly.

He was so small, she says.

We didn't know any better, she says.

We weren't married. We said we were. This was in Sheffield. When Sean was working in the place where they made the forks and spoons. I found out that a baby would be coming. I wanted to come home. I didn't want to raise a baby in that place. The way we were treated. Some did, I know, but if you could manage it at all, you'd get out of it. And Sean's uncle lived at Caherconlish. He wasn't well. Didn't have long. Said we were welcome with him, if we needed somewhere until we got on our feet. He knew I was the way I was and not married, but he had little time for the priests, so he passed no heed. There's room for ye here. So we came back. No-one even knew we were home we spent that much time looking after the patient. And cleaning up his house. Oh, the condition of it. Cats everywhere. If I wasn't nursing the poor man, I was cleaning up cat mess. Six weeks later he was gone. The uncle. Martin, his name was. And three months after that, Jude arrived. Jude.

Jude, she says.

A small angel, she says.

But he was never right, she says. Cats. Bad cess to them.

The girl, Tara says; Mrs Lynch?

She doesn't answer.

The girl, Tara tries again.

Mrs Lynch. Anne.

Still she doesn't answer.

Annie, will you answer the girl! It is the quiz man. On the television guide. Annie, he says again. His hair is moving. In the breeze. Annie, love. Now he is using Sean's voice. Annie, will ye don't be so rude. The Guards are here. Will ye talk to them.

She looks up. Looks at the smart alec. His arms still crossed. Looks at the girl, Tara. Her knees still together. A good girl, she thinks.

Do you have any babies? she asks.

Mrs Lynch, she says. Then; babies? No. No, I don't.

You should, she says. A baby is a gift. For a woman.

Well, maybe someday.

I had four, she says.

Four babies grew in me. Four came out of me, she says. And landed in the world. Now there's only three. I don't see them now, of course. Or their babies. I'm not let.

Mrs Lynch, says the man. I'm going to have to get you to answer some questions. What was found in the garden at Caherconlish; Jude, you say. Who was Jude? Was Jude yours?

She can't hear him. She is under the water. Down, down, down. Where it is so cold, she will never be warm again. Let me hold on to him, she says to it. Its eyes wide, its attention on the tiny thing in her arms, a gaping hole breathing its foul stench. Let me have him, she says, for one minute more.

Please, she says. She looks at the child. He is all hope. The light goes out.

Mrs Lynch, the girl says. Anne, what happened with Jude?

The floor was wet, she says. I was making a soda cake and I saw water on the floor. Sean, I says, shouted probably. The baby is coming. Don't you be daft, he says, there's no baby coming. Tis not time. Then a pain that tore me asunder. And the world was new. Jude was in it.

This was when exactly? says the man.

But he was small, she says. Sean's hand was bigger. And he wouldn't stop being blue coloured. I never heard him make a sound. The whole night long. Not a meg. In the morning he was cold.

Are you there, love? he says.

No, I'm not here, she says. Their little joke.

It is Sean. He is home. He is standing in the door frame. He is still handsome, she thinks. She looks at him. He looks back.

The girl, Tara stands and takes a small step towards Sean. The man looks at his watch and speaks into a black thing at his shoulder. The girl, Tara says words to Sean. He says words back. Their mouths are moving. No sounds are coming out. A minute or a month later a blue light sweeps across the room. She looks over her shoulder. Through the nets she sees a car pull up. The light stops and two new ones get out. No uniforms, not even a shirt and tie.

Sean is still in the door frame. She is still on the two-seater. There is no one else. His eyes on her. Her eyes on him. All words in that look.

The child was ours, she thinks. It was just us. And him. No one knew he was coming. No one knew when he went. We didn't want to share him. When there had been so little of him. Sean dug the hole. And afterwards we looked at it. A small mound.

Thin Coating
by Grace Keating

Longlisted for the Edinburgh Award for Flash Fiction 2021

R ime. Ice. Cold surface.
The girl walks home after the Saturday dance at the school on a freezing, winter night. Cries, half-syllables, half-breaths, mix in with the sound of a dog bark and the crunch of snow under her feet. The boy with his tongue stuck to a metal signpost grunts at her with pleading eyes. She walks to the end of his block to get his mother or his father.

She wakes them but can't get them to leave the house. The mother hands her a glass of water. Warm water to pour on the pole. Free the boy.

The following weekend, when she walks into the local hang-out, someone comes over and hands her a soda.

"I'll buy you a game, c'mon," he says, guiding her to the pool table.

As she walks from one side of the hall to the other, people part and smile, she hears whispers. Then, "A toast," he calls out, "To Lizzy, who saved my little brother."

And there she is, as famous for a day as anyone can get. For freeing the boy with his tongue stuckto the metal pole, on a cold pitch-black Saturday dance night.

Why wouldn't the mom or the dad come to help? She walked him back, saw him safely in, returned the glass and continued on her way home.

Rime, thin coating of ice. Thin coating of mom, thin coating of dad.

Impression, sunrise
by Jake Kendall

Longlisted, Scottish Arts Club Short Story Competition 2021

The boy made his way across the dark and colourless beach. His heart beat fast though his progress was slow. He stepped cautiously over slick jagged stones and around the glimmering outlines of silvery rock pools. His boots were handed down from his older brother. They were well-worn by now, their many tears and perforations unable to prevent the residual seawater of the shrinking tide from seeping into the fabric of his socks and chilling his feet.

He stopped by the outline of the jetty where the fishing boats were tied. He pulled his threadbare coat close to protect himself against the biting cold of the pre-dawn morning, his breath emerging in small puffs of warm mist that were swallowed swiftly by the night.

The boy was completely alone on the seafront. Likely all of Normandy was sleeping. He knew that he should be too, chasing lucid memories and fancies from the safety of his bedsheets. Soon he heard the distant declarations of the church clock as it chimed four times. His stomach and throat tightened. He could see it now, a solitary light, a distant orange orb, floating down from the cottages to join him on the beach.

The man holding it was not from the village. The boy had watched him keenly the day before, entreating the fishermen on their return to shore. The stranger had been wearing clothes quite unlike any the boy had seen before: frilly and delicate, they were alien artefacts belonging to another world entirely, an urbane life far removed from salt, spray and fresh-gutted fish. The boy had felt he could catch a phantom glimpse of distant Paris in those clothes, he could almost smell money on the man.

The stranger's approaches to the fishermen had seemed unsuccessful. He cut a disappointed figure as he left the beach and traipsed back towards the village. The boy raced after him to query his purpose, learning that the stranger wanted to be taken onto the water under darkness and was prepared to pay twenty francs to any person willing to do so.

The boy's father had fallen from a ladder while repairing their rooftop. He had broken his left leg and been bedridden for nearly five weeks. His father was a skilled fisherman, but the inexperience of his sons had shown while working the waters in his stead. Their catches were insufficient to live off, let alone sell. The family had already exhausted what meagre savings they once had and were living like scavengers. Their mother was feeding them using charitable offerings from the villagers, supplemented by seaweed, garden snails, garlic and mushrooms foraged from the woods nearby.

Too often the boy had seen his parents go to bed hungry so their children could eat. He had informed the wealthy stranger that seven of his thirteen years had been spent out on the cove and had insisted upon his ability to deliver safe passage as any. The man had looked him up and down. With a smile and a ruffle of the boy's hair, he said to meet at the jetty just after four that morning.

The orange orb neared. The boy spied a shadowed face peering out from behind a gas lantern. Something was attached to the man's back, a large bundle that was covered and strapped. As he approached the jetty the stranger called out a salutation in a voice soft and uncertain. The boy summoned his courage and replied in kind, waving his arm out to draw the man's attention.

Despite the strangers' eagerness to take immediately to the sea, the boy held out his hand, making a faltering request for payment before they took to the water. When the twenty francs were accounted for, the boy stepped onto the jetty. He forewarned the stranger of the looseness of the fourth board, not because the board was loose, but because it occurred to him that such instruction might lend an appearance of deep familiarity with the jetty and, by implication, the entire cove around them.

He found the familiar outline of the family boat, bobbing with the lapping waves. Having never removed its fastenings in the dark before, the boy asked for the gas lantern to be raised above the mooring post as he began unpinning and untying the ropes. He apologised silently to his family as he did so. They would be deeply worried to discover him gone. If his father found the strength to stand later, he might even reward the enterprise by thrashing the boy with leathers until the skin on his back broke – though, hopefully, the sight of twenty francs might assuage his father's fury.

The boy held the ropes and took hold of the gaslight with his free hand. He ushered the stranger onto the boat and watched as the man removed the bundle from his back and placed it gingerly onboard. The boy then passed the stranger the gaslight and climbed onto the outwards-facing bench. He took an oar and pushed them off the jetty and moved them through the rippling water, away from the shoreline, to where the pallid pewter water met the star-speckled sky.

The boy grunted and strained with each slow stroke. He pushed the boat starboard, where the cove was deepest, offering tacit prayers that nothing would catch and breach the keel. His right eye pooled with tears in the cold air, they stung the skin as they streamed impassively down one side of his face.

His passenger said nothing. The gas lantern flickered at their feet between them, illuminating them both from below. The inky countenance of the stranger seemed almost sinister; a partially concealed face, hovering, disembodied in the dark. He was relatively young, around thirty perhaps. His face was framed by a thin strip of facial hair that descended from his temples, around his chin and up to his bottom lip in a neat line. The small moustache that sat above his lips was imperfect, thicker at the corners of his mouth than it was under his nose. His thick black hair was slicked back to emerge again from behind his ears. A long coat was draped loosely over his shoulders, covering his entire body.

The boy's gaze lingered too long. The stranger caught the look and returned it, his dark eyes shining with some indecipherable, burning purpose. The boy found his mind involuntarily recalling stories read by his schoolteachers of that vengeful revenant called Monte Cristo.

"Do you like the night?" asked the stranger.

The question sent shivers down the boy's spine. His family's dire situation had made him rash. He had not truly stopped to consider who this man was and what his purpose could be out on these waters. He saw the stranger briefly as a vampire, one intent on luring a hapless victim out beyond the reach of civilisation, where escape was impossible. More likely, the stranger was mortal: an assassin, a pirate, or a smuggler. Perhaps the boy was inadvertently abetting an act of treason, or a vital mission to support some secret cause. Perhaps the mysterious bundle protected so preciously by the stranger was filled with money, jewels, or some other substances that could be traded with another boat. Who knew, the stranger might harbour no intentions of returning to the village at all – or leaving a living witness. They might spot a second vessel on the horizon. There might be no warning then, just a blade ran across the throat.

"I like the night," the stranger continued wistfully to fill the silence. "The colours! But sadly, it is quite impossible." His voice was articulate and refined, yet his base accent remained Northern French – likely the stranger hailed from a place not far from the boy's own village.

The boy kept rowing. "Where are we going?" he asked after a while.

"Take me there," the stranger replied, pointing towards a

limestone arch that protruded just outside the cove.

When they reached the place indicated by the stranger, the sun had sent out its first overtures to the day, ringing the eastern horizon with a luminous pale strip. The stranger reached into his pocket and produced an ornate silver pocket watch. He then took tentatively to his feet.

"Can you keep us still?" he asked.

"I will do my best," said the boy in a voice small and tremulous.

"Good enough," the stranger replied. "Apologies, this will take some time."

"What are we doing out here?" the boy forced himself to ask.

"We are here to capture something," the man said softly.

It was an answer ripe with intrigue. New possibilities still came rushing unbidden into the boy's mind. Perhaps the national authorities might reward any reports of illicit behaviour on the English Channel. Perhaps he might even find himself positioned to double-cross the stranger and have his family paid twice-over. These were possibilities that could perhaps favour the boy, presuming, of course, that his life was not sacrificed on the altar of whatever grim purpose had compelled his enigmatic passenger to ride this paltry vessel across the treacherous nocturnal waves.

Beneath the long coat, the stranger was wearing dark overalls, not unlike those worn by the village fishmongers. He began working the straps and fastenings of his bundle and produced a long, dark instrument. The boy found himself crying aloud for his mother, half-expecting to be struck. The stranger looked up and regarded the boy with wry silent amusement. Placing the object between them, the stranger pulled it out onto three legs before producing, not a telescope, nor a gun, but a blank white square and mounted it on top of the tripod.

"We have come out here to capture ..." the stranger added

in a breezy drawl "... the rising sun."

Several brushes and metallic tubes followed the tripod out from the bundle. The boy's sense of deep dread rapidly dissolved. After everything, his stranger was merely an artist!

"Absurd, isn't it?" the stranger exclaimed, squeezing paint out onto a slate palette, "to think people choose to sleep through such colours!" His amusement at the thought appeared to be quite genuine.

The boy was stupefied. Indeed, it was absurd: the boy had risked the fury of his family, their boat and even his life – all so some reckless poseur could make a painting of the sunrise – absurd was far too small a word! A host of obscenities formed in his mind. Were it clearly best not to provoke the insane, the boy would have aimed a furious eruption of relieved outrage in the direction of the lunatic sharing his boat. He held his tongue instead and sulked in silence.

"Have you ever witnessed such a sight?" asked the stranger, nodding back to the horizon.

The boy had indeed seen the daybreak before. He said so bluntly, finding himself in no mood to indulge the saccharine whimsy of a sophomoric dandy with little regard for human life.

"Your eyes are closed, my young friend," the stranger insisted as he commenced his work. "Nature opened mine. She taught me how to see ... Look again."

The boy shook his head and turned his attention back east. They would float there for hours, the stranger painting like a man possessed, the boy thinking that he should probably take him to the nearest asylum the very moment they landed. Nevertheless, the boy eventually conceded – privately at least – that in some ways he was glad to have been shown such a vision.

He had indeed seen the daybreak before, but never one such as this. He saw the morning sun, resplendent in a magnificent shade of deep coral red, rising like God's own gas

132

lantern to peel back the darkness and reveal the vibrant splendour of the world once again. He experienced the world as a haze of mottled vaporous light and found himself immersed completely amidst an exquisite symphony of orange, salmon and violet that danced together on the waters and mingled with the mist.

Pickles and Jam
by Kathryn Barton

Longlisted for the Edinburgh Award for Flash Fiction 2021

I've been wretchedly ill. Wretched and retching. Staggering from bedroom to bathroom. By the time I recovered, the day and I were too spent to do anything but crawl back to bed.

Today: sun; blue sky; birds singing and me singing with them. Not sick. The urge to dress, to go out, to shop. Nearly lunch time and I want to eat. Oh, how I want to eat. The supermarket has wonderful aisles full of produce.

Home, the ingredients spread out. Bread, healthily beige, studded with seeds like a parrot's celebration. Spread – plant-based. A momentary pang for the mouth-feel of creamy butter, thick-layered, with the tang of salt. Strawberry jam, the label promising ripe, juicy fruits packed shoulder to shoulder. All too often it's a sugar liquid with a few squashed entities. But I paid for the best, I'm dribbling at the thought of biting into a boiled and candied strawberry. My teeth stand to attention at the next jar. Acid green juice enriching the long, dark fingers of the gherkins.

Bread on the sacrificial altar of my bread board. Spread with spread. Mash strawberries into the creamy depths. Pickles, green added to yellow and red, a tapestry to delight the senses. Another slice of jammed bread. Press firmly.

Pickles and jam sandwich clasped in both hands. Sandwich? Oh, no. This is a symbol, a milestone, a trumpeted hallelujah, a wondrous, wondrous thing.

After the years of empty longing, this is the first craving of my first pregnancy.

What William is talking about
by Michael Callaghan

Longlisted, Scottish Arts Club Short Story Competition 2021

The landline started to ring as Amanda was opening the front door. She almost didn't bother answering. Chances where it was someone telling her she was the lucky recipient of a double-glazing promotion, or asking about a recent road traffic accident that she never had. But she did answer, dropping her shopping bags on the floor and grabbing the receiver just in time.

"Hello?"

"Dr Amanda Scanlon?" A male voice.

"Yes, who ...?"

"Sergeant Taylor. Sanderton Police Station."

Amanda froze for a moment. Her mind leapt to her fifteen-year-old daughter Charlotte – dropped off at dance class an hour earlier – and to her husband Robert who was flying back from his New York business trip right now. *Had something ...?*

But Taylor continued.

"We have someone in custody. He's 15 years old. He needs psychiatric assessment. Can you attend?"

She relaxed. Just the job. But she wasn't on duty.

"I'm not on call Sergeant. It's Dr James Colclough who's on. Have you tried ...?"

"Ah – yes. We would have. Except ... this kid specifically requested you. Says he knows you. His name's William Magee? He's in your daughter's class at school?"

William Magee? It rang a vague bell but nothing concrete. And *requested* her? That was a new one. Psychiatric assessments of youths going through the criminal justice system was her bread and butter and had been for twenty years. Usually it was to assess suicide risk or confirm their fitness to plead. But she had never had one *ask* for her. She considered. The station was only five minutes away. James was probably on the golf course by now. And if this boy had asked for her, that suggested he would actually talk to her. Which he might not to James. Getting these kids to talk was often half the battle.

"Okay. I'll come. Can you tell me what this is about?"

There was a pause. A sigh.

"I'd rather do that at the station, Dr Scanlon"

She arrived within ten minutes. The uniform at the desk immediately ushered her through to an interview room where Sergeant Taylor was sitting, at one side of a desk, holding an iPhone. Taylor was mid-fifties, with thinning hair and a spreading waist that suggested his duties were more desk based than in the field. He looked troubled – pale and sweating a little.

"All very cloak and dagger Sergeant ..." she said as she sat opposite him.

He sighed. "Yeah, well, perhaps you'll understand when you see this."

He pressed a key on the iPhone and turned it towards her.

A video was playing. It was slightly jumpy but clear enough. It showed a boy sitting on a park bench. She recognised the boy – it was Reilly Devlin, a classmate of Charlotte. Sitting beside Reilly on the bench was a golden Labrador and Reilly had one arm draped round it. She knew – with a sudden, dreadful, premonition – what was going to happen. And it did. The dog's head jolted back and partly exploded in a horrifying burst of blood and bone and fur.

She clasped her hand to her mouth.

Taylor took back the phone. "Pretty much my reaction."

"Charlotte ... told me that Reilly's dog had been ... but

136

..."

"Yeah. His parents reported it of course. We didn't think we would get who did it. Lot of sickos out there. But twenty minutes ago, this kid came in. Said he wanted to confess. Made me watch this video. Then said he knew he would be arrested and knew he would be given a mental health assessment. And ... requested you. His parents, maybe not coincidentally, are both out of town." He shook his head, as if trying to rid himself of what he had just seen. "Never seen the like. And I've been a cop for thirty years. Where did he even get that gun? But anyway ... can you speak to him?"

Amanda sat down opposite William, placing her phone on the desk, and studied him. He had brown curly hair, was neatly dressed in smart school uniform and was sitting straight, hands on his knees. She had only the vaguest of recollections of him, probably from of the school shows or a class photo. She couldn't recall Charlotte ever mentioning him.

"Good afternoon, Dr Scanlon." His voice seemed calm, assured. "Let me say right away, I admit it. I did it."

Amanda was taken aback. Talking about the actual crime, when one had been committed, was something she normally avoided.

"William, you must know, your discussions with me are confidential, but not ... privileged. If this were to go to court, I would have to let them know what you say. So ..."

He nodded. "I understand. But I *did* it. And I want to say *why* I did it."

Amanda considered. Teenagers typically stared at their shoes. Getting a grunt could be an achievement. William wanted to talk. She decided she would let him talk.

She sat back, unfolding her notebook and clicking her pen. "All right, William. Tell me what happened." She thought, however, that she could guess the unfolding tale. A story about daily, relentless, bullying by this Reilly. A slow burning fuse of rage that one day exploded in that act of horrifying revenge.

William smiled. "It really is so good to be finally able to talk. Now in films, psychiatrists say to their patients, tell me about your childhood. Is that right?"

"Well ... not necessarily ..."

"Ah. Well, I will anyway. You see, when I was little, I was fascinated with the concept of life. My mum told me once that the ground under my feet was full of insects and seeds and microbes. That really struck me. I used to spend long summer hours lying back on our garden lawn, imagining the whole wondrous canopy of life underneath me. It filled me with ... awe."

She nodded. Not what she was expecting and she couldn't see where it was going. But not particularly abnormal. Then her phone buzzed, indicating an incoming message. William glanced at it.

"Are you going to get that?"

"No. I want to listen to you William. Carry on."

He smiled.

"Alright. Anyway, I used to think how wonderful it would be to *create* life. But of course I couldn't. And that ... frustrated me. I realised I would never get that power. Of being ... God. And so do you know what eventually my mind turned to Dr Scanlon?"

"No ..."

"Destroying it.

"Destroy ...?"

"Yes. If you can't be God, the next best role is the Devil, right? It started with plants. One day, I ripped up my mother's roses from the ground. She was furious of course. But I wasn't sorry. It gave me such a luxurious feeling of ... *power*. But of course they were just plants. So I moved on, to insects and spiders. I would find them in the garden and crush them with my fingers. And it so ... *pleased* me Dr

138

Scanlon. It was *much* better than plants. I could feel the cracking and splintering and bursting of their little legs and eyes as I pushed my fingers against them. It felt … *intoxicating*."

Her phone buzzed again. Again she ignored it. Things were definitely getting weirder now, she thought. Still, childhood cruelty like this was far from an unknown phenomenon.

"But eventually, that wasn't enough," said William. "I moved onto to … bigger animals. I caught a frog in the garden and crushed it. Bashed it against the wall. Watched it *explode*. It was better. But still … something missing. Then I realised. It was all very well to destroy God's work. But God didn't appear and let me know how unhappy he was! I realised I needed … well, not an audience per se … but to see the results of what I had achieved reflected by another creature's reaction. You understand?"

"I'm … not sure I do, William …"

"I'll clarify. I was walking in woods nears my home. I came across a nest of mice. A mother and babies. I took up a rock smashed it down on those baby mice. And I saw the pain and confusion and despair in the mother as she tried to come to terms with what had happened. I have never felt so euphoric! I remember thinking …" – at this point he shook his fists in the air and affected an American accent – "*… that's what I'm talking about!*" He lowered his hands and smiled. His face had got paler, his pupils had dilated and his breathing had become shallow.

Her phone buzzed again, twice, in quick succession. This time she hardly noticed it.

William sighed and continued. "But I'm afraid … even that wasn't enough. I wanted *more*. And I decided that domestic cats were a suitable step up. They are often docile and unafraid of humans and, more importantly, have a *human being* who loves them. The girl next door, Angela, had a cat called Ginger. A nice cat. Rubbed its head against your leg if it saw you. One day I saw him come out and I called him. He came over happily and I killed him with my mum's iron poker – it took four strikes to finish the job – then left him by the side of the road so it would look like a car accident. Then I hid behind a tree, until Angela came out looking for Ginger, calling for him ... Can you imagine, Dr Scanlon? My anticipation of her reaction when she found him ... and when she did ..."

Amanda thought of Charlotte's beloved cat, Scout. *If anything like that ever happened ...*

"... that's what I'm *talking* about!" said William again. "It was so *wonderful* to see her torment. To feel that *power*, not of life, no, but of *death*. How potent that power was! But you see, Dr Scanlon, how I had to move on again. And how I came to do what I did to Reilly's dog. I know Reilly loved that dog – he talked about nothing else at school – and that, of course, was the very point. I planned it meticulously. I was able to get a suitable shooting device from the internet – it really is amazing what you can purchase if you're thorough enough. I practised beforehand using my gun with one hand and filming with the other. And it all proceeded so well! When I saw Reilly's face crumple like that, I thought ..." and again he raised his fists and shook them. "That's what I'm *talking* about ..."

Amanda's phone buzzed and buzzed. And buzzed again.

William sighed again. Lowered his fists. "I knew, of course, that I couldn't go on. Part of me knew. I deserved to be caught. Punished. And so – I wanted to go out with a bang."

"And ... Reilly's dog was the ... bang ...?" Her voice was barely a whisper. She thought she saw. She thought she understood.

But William shook his head.

"Oh *no!* That was just a *dog*. I wanted the ultimate thrill.

140

Something more than someone's pet, however loved. And so … that's why I did it.

"Did it …?"

"I went to Churchill Street in the West End today. For my last … indulgence."

"Churchill Street." Something cold and clammy seemed to press against her. "I was …"

"There, yes. You dropped off Charlotte outside the underpass. I watched you drive off. I remember thinking – Charlotte is such a pretty girl. And so full of … joy. I watched her get closer. She actually smiled when she saw me standing there. Because she's kind like that. And then … well, you've guessed what happened, haven't you? And what I did afterwards?"

Her phone buzzed yet again. William looked again at it.

"Are you sure you aren't going to get that, Dr Scanlon?"

And this time, she did pick it up. Dimly, she heard footsteps running down the corridor outside. She opened the message and there was attachment. A video. As if in a trance and, just as the door crashed open, she pressed play.

"Now that's what I'm *talking* about…" said William happily.

Judgement
by Lorraine Queen

Shortlisted for the Edinburgh Award for Flash Fiction 2021

I'd got Mum some lovely flowers from Marks and decided to leave the car and walk as it was so rare to have sunshine on Mother's Day. She's not been up here very long and I hadn't realised how steep this hill was, so I was taking it slow and watching my feet. I heard them just before I got to the turn. I edged forward. Four of them were about fifty yards away, shouting and pushing each other. I saw their Celtic scarves and what looked like a small bottle being handed round. I needed to pass them to get to Mum's, but thought it better to wait and see if they moved on.

Soon three of them headed off towards a car parked further down. The last one stayed leaning against the stone for support. After a minute or two one of the boys in the car opened the door and shouted.

'Hey Stevie! C'mon, we need to go.'

When they had driven off, I walked down to Mum's and as I passed where they had been, I saw the small bottle of vodka, a packet of cigarettes and the Celtic scarf still lying there. I stopped to read the inscription.

Michael Aaron Docherty
Taken suddenly 13th September 2019
Dearly loved son of Alan and Mhairi
Twin brother to Steven
Forever in our hearts.

A New Life
by Stewart Paterson

Longlisted, Scottish Arts Club Short Story Competition *2021*

Jackie sat along the top of the steel bench, hunched and alone. His feet on the seat below, his face hidden inside a zipped-up parka hood, his shoulders crouched over, his head almost touching his knees. The sky turned to dark and the air in the street grew colder. He shivered as he thought about the following day and where he might be the same time. He had no idea. At his feet were rough scratchings into the bright red paint. All his pals' initials, scraped out in square silver letters, but not his.

He remembered when they had done it. They had huddled round, as each took their turn with the screwdriver held in their clenched fists, smiling at their work, passing the tool around.

'Nah. Fuck that. A'm no a vandal,' he said when it was offered to him.

'Shitebag,' they laughed, as he walked away.

Jackie had hardly seen those pals in months. Ever since he started going out with Lisa he would stop, only briefly, on his way to hers while they played football. The game would pause.

'Ye playin', Jackie?'

'Nah, no the night, boys.'

'Ye away tae see yer wee burd, Jackie?' The swooning voices mocked.

'Aye. Ye jealous?'

He would walk on and away, up the hill, and the thud of the ball against the gable end fading behind him. Just months before it was Jackie who would turn up first with the ball ready to start a game, wearing his Scotland top or one of the many other replica shirts he had pestered his ma for money to buy. Hours later, on his way home, if they were still hanging around at the benches, he would stop. The football long over, and boredom settling in for the rest of the night, they would soon start to probe for what he had Lisa had been up to earlier.

'Fuck off, pricks.' And he was on his way home, leaving them again.

His parka hood swivelled left and right, as he peered out into the night. He pressed the light button on his digital watch and the numbers glowed green. He knew he should be home by now but he was waiting for as long as possible. The curtains were drawn on the rows of tenement windows facing him, little skelves of light sneaking out from where night owls were still up. He stared down at his white trainers, tomorrow on his mind.

The day before, Lisa had told him that her ma knew.

'Whit did she say?

'She just touched my belly and said "Have you got something to tell me, hen?" an A just burst oot greetin.'

Lisa was kept off school and taken to the doctors. That evening, just hours earlier, Jackie and Lisa sat silently, side by side, her da staring at Jackie but more with sadness than the anger he had been braced for. Jackie had expected, feared, an explosion, rage, violence even. Instead, he got silence, an intimidating, unsettling silence. Then the plans started. Plans were being made. Made for Lisa. Plans to speak to a guidance teacher, the head teacher, doctors again, he heard about clinics and people he had never heard about before, health visitors and family planning. He stared at the faces making the plans, nodding slowly from time to time, when he thought he was expected to, while he thought about other plans, plans that only involved him. Then he shuddered back into the moment when it was decided Lisa's mother would phone Jackie's mother and arrange for her and Lisa's da to visit his ma and da. And in an instant, she was up and out of the sofa. Jackie looked at Lisa and listened hard to the silence coming from her da.

For weeks he had dreaded this day, when it all becomes real for him. Every night he had lain awake, staring at patterns in the polystyrene mosaic ceiling tiles, shapes forming, then disappearing above his head. The occasional distant rumble of overnight lorries on the main road a strangely comforting sound. At the same hour each night the noise of a freight train came in, got louder and took a minute before it faded back, leaving the silence again. Jackie thought of where the lorries were going and where the train's journey might end. He lay on his back, deep into the night, wondering what would happen to him. Would the school throw him out? Would the police come for him? He had heard that boys got charged and he thought he would probably be sent to a home.

The moon disappeared, swallowed by clouds, and the only light was from the orange street lamps. One was blinking and buzzing above his head and another was completely out. He could tell Mrs Logan, next door to his pal Robbie, was watching him from behind a curtain. He muttered to himself …

'Nosy auld cow, ye gonnae phone the polis for some'dy sittin oan a bench.'

Jackie knew if he was at the meeting of the mas and das, more plans would be made. Plans made for him. He could hear them already.

'Well, you should have thought about that …'

'You've made your bed, boy …'

It was what worried him most. What would people say, what would happen? When they were together in Lisa's bedroom they worried together, about them. What they were going to do. What would happen to them? But on the walks home from Lisa's at night through the darkening streets, he felt alone. He worried what would happen to him.

What were they going to do to him? What was he going to do?

He stared down at his trainers and thought he would need a new pair soon. He felt into his inside pocket and took out the Abbey National junior savers book he had been carrying with him for the last week. He opened it and looked at his balance for at least the tenth time that week. He had £38.50 saved from his paper round. He knew he had more than enough for the bus fare to London, or somewhere else.

He had looked up Buchanan Bus Station in the phone book when no-one else was at home.

'How was it always London people ran away to. How no somewhere else?' he wondered but then wondered 'where else was there?'

He remembered watching *Sportsnight*, the week before, a midweek game, Aston Villa were playing Liverpool in an FA Cup replay and the English commentator said it was at Villa Park in Birmingham. The places of other teams he saw on television came into his head. He had never thought of them as real places, but they must be. Nottingham, Norwich, Manchester, Leeds. He knew they were places and others like Tottenham, Chelsea, Everton were places in places.

He asked the woman on the phone how much it was for a ticket to London then how much to Birmingham and how much to Liverpool. That was the full extent of his plan. Get on a bus at Buchanan Street, then get off somewhere else, somewhere far away, somewhere where no-one knew him. In another city where no-one would find him and no-one would put him in a home. He jumped down from the bench and slouched home, one worn *Hi-Tec* trainer in front of the other.

He was barely inside the door when his ma was out in the hall, asking why Lisa's ma and da were coming. He knew she would have been waiting to hear his key rattle around in the lock.

He lied. 'They just want to meet youse cos me and Lisa have been going out for ages an A'm always roon at hers.'

'Hmm. Naw. Naw, naw, naw', she slowly shook her head. Her narrowed eyes followed him as he slipped past and into his room. He shut the door, kicked his trainers off, hung up his parka on the knob on the outside of the wardrobe, flicked off the big light and lay on the bed and stared into the darkness.

In the morning, he went to school as normal and was late as normal. Lisa was to be kept off again and Jackie was to go round at lunchtime. The bell rang at half 12, he put on his parka, walked out the school gates and ran to the bank on the main street. He handed over the book and asked to take out all but £1 of the cash in his account and crossed the street to the bus stop to go into town. Upstairs, he sat near the back, watching for anyone who might know him getting on. Every head that popped up through the spiral stairwell filled him with dread. When the bus got to the stop nearest his street he looked down, scanning the queue for anyone who might ask where he was going. He saw Robbie's big brother waiting to get on. He would be going to his work in the record shop in the town. He tried to think of an excuse for where he was going and wanted to hide under the seat so he wouldn't be spotted. Instead, he bent down pretending to be looking his PE bag for something, until the bus moved off. No-one came upstairs. He waited until the bus was slowing right down at his stop before getting up, jumping down the stairs, and rushing off just before the driver shut the doors, before anyone could see him.

Jackie stood in a long queue at the ticket office, with £38 in his pocket and his PE bag at his feet filled with socks, pants, a pair of denims, his other jacket and his good shoes. A bus for Birmingham left the station at 2pm and he worked out he would be there by the time the mas and das were sat together. In front of him, a big West Indian woman towered over a little girl clutching a small, worn teddy bear. The girl was sobbing quietly and pressing her face into the woman's long, bright multi-coloured, patterned skirt. The rest of the queue was looking at them a big bundle of colour in among a sea of grey. She stroked the girl's hair and told her they would be home in time for tea with grandma, as she kept two large laundry bags close to her feet. Jackie listened to her loud but soothing tones calming the little girl.

As he stared at the woman and her daughter, Jackie thought of Lisa and how she was just as terrified as him. She would be sitting, watching the clock, wondering why he had not come at lunchtime, like he said he would. The queue moved and the woman shuffled forwards, nudging the bags along with her big feet in big brown sandals, the girl still clinging to her skirt. He could picture Lisa sitting in the kitchen, looking out the window waiting for him. He knew she was just as scared of the plans her ma was making as he was. She was already terrified of everybody at school knowing. Outside a white National Express bus pulled into the stance. The driver changed the sign in the window from Glasgow to London via Birmingham.

'Aw fuck', he said, too loudly.

The woman turned sharply, ready to scold him, but he had already picked up his bag and was running out of the station.

Lucky
by Ann MacLaren

Shortlisted for the Edinburgh Award for Flash Fiction 2021

First time lucky, Dolly! Haven't I always said it pays to take a gamble? You'll need to be careful though, it's not a fortune. But of course, you can splash out a bit. Treat yourself. Yes, I know it was your ticket! I'm just trying to help. I know what you're like – you'll want to spend it on the family, spoil them. They won't thank you for it. Oh, a new car, is it? Your old one's fine, it's not as if you go anywhere. Anyway, they're all computerised nowadays, you'd find it very confusing. Tell you what … I could put half of it away for you, somewhere safe. Your own wee nest egg, it'll be there when you need it. No, I won't put it on a horse! Of course, if the right one was running, if a dead cert was whispered in my ear, I could double your money. Know what I'm saying? But I'm not asking for a penny for myself. Nothing. It's all yours. Though I know you wouldn't grudge me something for a wee bet. Share and share, eh? Listen, Dolly, we can talk about it later. Let's go round to Malone's and celebrate, just the two of us. Maybe have a meal … you won't want to be cooking after a couple of glasses of Prosecco. Or, Champagne, it's entirely up to you. Then we'll have an early night, eh? It's been a while. Here's your jacket, Dolly. Don't forget your purse.

Fair Exchange is No Robbery
by Anthony McGuinness

Longlisted, Scottish Arts Club Short Story Competition 2021

The mercy of God there wasn't so much blood and the poor thing didn't suffer as far as I can say but the worst of it was I hadn't the flipping foggiest *who* the unfortunate creature belonged to like there wasn't any sort of an ID around its neck or what have you but I reckoned it must have been a local because I swear I seen a very similar looking child about the place tramping on the flower beds in front of the apartments which is absolutely against the rules in my opinion and I happen to pay attention to the flower beds or rather Gillian does because there is a slug issue and she tried it with the home remedies for a bit but it's quite unsightly isn't it eggshells in the flowerbeds so the next thing she tried was the green pellets out of her own pocket and all which worked a treat in fairness but then you do get millions of flies so you do because of all the dead slugs but that is all by the by

Gillian reckons I must have been distracted late for work back of the shirt collar wet no breakfast into the van rummaging about under the seat for the little tub of pear-drops but there wasn't any pear-drops so there wasn't all that was left was the sugar in the bottom of the tub and the next thing I remember was reversing and then didn't I hear the bump so out I get and there he was or she was I'm not sure I didn't check to be honest there it was behind the rear wheel on the passenger side I am a very experienced driver and there is definitely a blind spot on those vans everybody says so believe you me

I was actually expecting something horrible and messy but it was still kind of almost perfect like you wouldn't even know it was dead apart from the eyes being closed and no

150

breath so I put my hand down and sort of rubbed its forehead or whatever it's called on a child but I knew immediately so I did but I wouldn't say it was stone dead because it was still warm but it *was* stone dead and I knew it was me who was after running it over so the first thing I did was stand up on my tippy-toes and see if I could see anybody I might know or if anyone seen what happened happening but I didn't see anyone so I didn't on the other hand I didn't want to leave the child just there do you know what I mean leaving a child on the road like that would not be on not for me No Sir I felt by rights I ought to find whoever was responsible for it and let them give it a decent burial or whatever but I really had to get on in to work I was desperate late already late as a doornail Gillian always says and there was the usual stock of bags in the back of the van the girls in the shop do use them for the gift items they are quite good quality bags actually and so I put the child into one and I must say these children can look quite sizeable when they are running around the place but this particular child was actually quite light and portable and the bag was an extra-large The Jumbos we call them with the twine handles deceptively strong so I put the bag in the van and then I drove on in to work and to be honest with you I did actually forget about the child

So anyway work you know yourself

Having said that I did come to think of it think about it a couple of times during the day between phone calls to the auditors and the franchise people because I wasn't too comfortable with the idea of the bag in the back of the van but I just told myself Look the car park is down in the basement and it's always fairly chilly in the basement and it wasn't like the van was sitting out in the sun then all of a sudden wasn't it four o'clock and Marguerite was calling to say she needed the van in the morning so I said Yes No Problémo so the upshot as they say was I would have to take the bus home in the evening which wouldn't be ideal really but I just told myself Look nobody is going to know what's in the bag like whenever you see a bloke with a gift-bag or whatever you never think Aye-aye there he goes with his dead child isn't that literally the last thing anyone would think

As it happens, I did need to get the few bits and bobs in town for Gillian there is a department store near the bus-stop that she does like though I would not agree with her on that point I do be slagging Gillian sometimes that she does be shopping like a Japanese Housewife which means a little bit every day apparently but she knows I am only teasing because she is really a great believer in the BIG SATURDAY SHOP but sometimes you just haven't an option sure you don't and I fully accept that

So at five o'clock I went down to the car park and I just put a couple of sheets of the beeswax paper over the top so you wouldn't see in if you were standing over it because the mouths of those bags do be fairly wide that is the way they are designed and off I went on my merry way

So wasn't I in the department store I was telling you about I won't name names and I had done the food shop in the basement a couple of things for myself twenty razors was the most expensive even though they were on special like that would be a whole year's supply practically and some tinned mackerel and three packets of nuts because Gillian is on paleo except for the pear-drops which I do give her sometimes in the car and then wasn't I up on the ground floor looking at a blue and black quilted gilet I wasn't even trying it on and the next thing didn't I turn around and somebody had made off with the messages as Gillian calls them now doesn't that take the biscuit needless to say I was annoyed and basically sort of astonished? And then I just thought Ha wide like there is no way they are getting away with this and the next thing wasn't I haring it down onto the

152

street pedestrianized fortunately and I knew my shopping would be easy to spot because there was the two smaller bags because I'd be a bit squeamish now about having my shopping in with anything dead and then there was the gift bag pink and black with the appliqué triangles apparently they are called and do you know what didn't I clock the bags at once I was thinking If you *are* going to steal another person's shopping Missus don't go for something so flipping conspicuous Oh Yes she must have thought it was a woman's shopping because of the pink but she had made a big blunder there let me tell you and I was surprised because she didn't look like an immigrant or what have you just a lady an ordinary lady I mean she could have been Gillian so she could and I thought about maybe going over and reefing the stuff back off of her but then that would have looked very dodgy altogether would it not these are the things you have to worry about as a man in this day and age so I hung back plus I suppose I sort of couldn't believe it just a lady out shopping after work really it is a perfect disguise for a criminal

So I hung back as I say across the street as she was browsing in the windows *or pretending to browse* and then she pulled herself up outside Millennium Sports looking up at the sky as if to see was it going to rain or maybe she was checking for the helicopter and I watched her peek into the plastic bags for to see what had she got in her lucky dip and then she lifted the big bag with one hand underneath and I could see her face was puzzled because it would have felt funny so it would and she reached in with the other hand and pulled aside the beeswax paper

And you can sort of imagine her seeing the dead child in the gift bag and didn't she faint

Now that did confuse me a bit at the time because it wasn't like it was *her* child

But down she went in anyways like a sack of spuds it

really was the mercy of God she didn't lash her skull off the pavement the door-man at Millennium Sports fair play to him he seen the whole thing whipped off his jacket rolled it up like a sausage stuffed it under the woman's head but she was still out cold so she was so out came the walkie-talkie and the ambulance was there in jig time a big kerfuffle pedestrians all stepping aside What's all this? the fellows in the ambulance they hooshed her up on the stretcher but they didn't give her The Baywatch or any of that so her vitals must have been tickety-boo

I still wanted my shopping I could see it just laying there on the ground but who would have believed me

Do you know what I'm saying

This is it isn't it

So they're just about to close the back doors of the ambulance when the security guard picks up the bags all three of them and bungs them up to the paramedic somebody told me these lads are all Fire Brigade but he didn't look like Fire Brigade to me and I could see him stowing the bags in a corner of the ambulance keeping them safe for your woman for when she wakes up in the hospital

And then the ambulance pulls away no siren but the lights were flashing so they were

I got the 339 straight home and I didn't bother going back for to buy the messages all over again and when I told Gillian she said Fair Exchange is No Robbery the mackerel and the nuts weren't all that important at the end of the day and it would have been a very unpleasant thing for me to have to do to bury the child myself very unpleasant to be perfectly honest with you

154

A Trackside Fairy Tale
by Julie Evans

Shortlisted for the Edinburgh Award for Flash Fiction 2021

And when I finally go to the place that you chose, the sun is out. Wildflowers stipple the sidings, cranesbills bounding pink from the grass. On the fence, a DANGER sign. A thousand dying shop-bought blooms are pinned and hung, severed stems protruding from cellophane, petals crushed inside the twists of wire.

They call it community mourning. Counsellors wait in classrooms. Mothers hold their children tight. *There but for the grace …* And you are the tiny green pea smothered under the mattresses of their imagined griefs. But I feel the shape of you. You black-and-blue me, kick against my diaphragm.

Once, pink-pyjamaed, you asked me for stories. 'Tell me a Once Upon a Time.' And I gave you a witch in every tale, hags climbing hair, offering a shiny apple, tempting with a gingerbread house. I thought witches were just figments, but here they are amongst the crowd. They are not old. They are children, come to snap the scene with their phones, their pocket instruments of torture. Old messages are deleted; new ones have appeared, clichés of angels and bright stars. Tell me, my beautiful girl, which ponytails are theirs? Whose nails tapped vitriol on glass? Whose mouths flashed curses between molar bands and arch wires?

What do I do? Perform my grief? Ululate?

Clear a path. Here she is: The Star of the Show.

And I hear your voice on the wind, echoing through the tunnel, travelling along the steel rails. 'Go home, Mum, you're embarrassing me.'

The Waiting Room
by Hilary Thain

Longlisted, Scottish Arts Club Short Story Competition 2021

Before I could close the door, the icy cold wound its way around the feet of the three occupants, followed by a flurry of snow dusting everything like icing sugar.

'Shut the door! It's Baltic!'

'I need a return to Glasgow please.'

'That'll be £2.40'.

I took a seat and enjoyed the embrace of the warm air from the overhead fan heater as I looked out at the snow slowly building up against the windows.

'It's Baltic oot there,' said the old guy sitting in the corner.

'Statin the bleedin obvious mate,' replied the young guy in the opposite corner.

'Phones are all down,' he announced as I pulled mine out. Shoving it back in my pocket I wondered to myself if the train was actually going to come.

'Must be snow on the towers or somethin'.'

'Train's late cos of the weather,' the old man informed me.

'The train's coming, it's just been held up,' came a voice from behind the desk.

'He's been telling us that for an hour now,' said the old lady sitting opposite me.

'Held up where?' enquired the old man.

'Down the line a bit, but it's coming.'

'How do you know it's coming?'

'Well trains always come. Well eventually they do, unless they crash, which is very unlikely. Pretty much as long as it doesn't derail it will make it to where it's going, maybe just take it a bit longer than it's supposed to.

'Well that's reassuring, last time it was leaves on the line.

How can leaves stop a train?'

'They don't stop the trains mam, just slow them down.'

'Would a pile of snow not stop a train?'

'Aye, for a bit, but the snow will melt or a snow plough will clear it, I tell you, a train always gets where it's going, maybe just not at the time it's supposed to.'

'I'm going to see ma girlfriend, it's her birthday today. Only I can't contact her, she'll be doin her nut,' the young man said.

'Aw, that's nice laddie, M&S are having a wee sale today, seemed like a good idea though now I'm not so sure,' said the old lady as she peered out through the fogged-up windows.

'None of us are going nowhere,' came the voice from behind the desk.

'I'm going to Glasgow,' the old man replied. 'I've got business I need to take care of.'

'I doubt it mate, at least not today.'

'I thought you said the train was coming.'

'Aye, and it is, just maybe not today'

'Could you not have told me that before I bought my ticket'

'At that point it looked likely the train would be coming.'

'That was 2 minutes ago'

'He's been sayin' the same thing for an hour now.'

'Are you saying the train's not coming now?'

'That's not what I said, I just said you're unlikely to be going to Glasgow today.'

'Could you not have said that when I was buying my ticket.'

'Like I said, at that point it was looking likely the train would make it through'.

'Look, I only bought my ticket two minutes ago and the train's over an hour late, why didn't you say something? What about the train that's due in five minutes?'

'Well that's stuck behind the train that was due an hour ago.'

'And where exactly is the train that was due an hour ago?'

'As I've been telling these guys, it's just down the line. It was making headway but the snow's getting worse, there's a chance it might not make it through anytime soon.'

'When will we know for sure,' the old lady wanted to know.

'Well, I'm not sure we'll ever know for sure.'

'Can you not phone the driver or something?'

'The phones are all down'.

'So you're telling us the train's not coming.'

'No, I'm telling you that it's maybe unlikely that it's coming.'

'So we should just go home.'

'Well maybe, don't want you getting home though, and then the train arrives.'

'Well I wouldn't know if I was home.'

'But I'd know, then I'd feel bad for telling you it wasn't coming.'

'What if it isn't coming?'

'Well then maybe you should go home.'

'I'm going nowhere, I've got business to take care of.'

'I've got to get to ma girlfriend, she'll kill me if I miss her birthday.'

'I don't want to miss out on all those bargains.'

After a silence that lasted some time, the young lad got up and headed for the door.

'You going home son?'

'I need a smoke, but I can't get the bleedin door open,' he said pushing against it. The old man moved over to add his heft to the mission but to no avail.

'Damn.'

'Looks like none of us are going anywhere then,' came the

voice from behind the desk.

'Bugger.'

We all sat in the waiting room not really sure what we were waiting for anymore.

'I killed somebody.'

Everyone turned to look at the old man sitting in the corner.

For what seemed like an eternity no one said anything.

I began to wonder if I'd just imagined it.

'Sure you did,' said the young lad eventually.

'Aye A did, it wis a mistake though, A'm no one of them serial killers.'

'Well I'm glad to hear it,' said the old lady.

'There's a number of people I'd like to kill,' came the voice from behind the desk.

'That's why I'm going tae Glasgow, need to sort out the body.'

'Where is it?' asked the young lad.

'Am no tellin ye son, next thing A know the polis'll be round askin questions.'

'But if it was an accident surely it's better to just come clean,' said the old lady.

The old man appeared to ponder this for a bit.

'Aye, well it depends how ye define accident.'

'How do you define accident?'

'Well, it's when ye dae sumthin that ye don't mean to dae.'

'Like when you eat three boxes of Mr Kipling Cherry Bakewell tarts all in one go,' came the voice from behind the desk.

'Like when you sleep wi your girlfriend's best pal when your girlfriend's away to her nan's funeral,' said the young lad at the same moment.

'Who's sleeping with tarts?' asked the old lady.

'It's nuthin like either of them things. Killin someone is

serious.'

'I'll say,' said the old lady, 'and it's a shame these tarts don't have more respect for themselves.'

'Tarts that you eat, not sleep with.'

'He's a cannibal?' she asked in horror.

'Look, he killed someone, he cheated on his girlfriend and I ate three boxes of Cherry Bakewell tarts,' came the explanation from behind the desk, 'no one is eating anyone!'

'Well that's a relief.'

'And young man, what way is that to treat your girlfriend?'

'It was an accident. I really didn't mean to. It just kinda happened. I've been feelin sick ever since trying to decide whether or no to tell her.'

'Honesty's the best policy son.'

'What you don't know won't hurt you.'

'Helpful. Real helpful, thanks. I need a smoke,' he said taking a tin from his pocket and opening it.

'Oi, there'll be no smoking in here.'

'Aw come on man, ma nerves are shot, it's helps with ma anxiety.'

'Let the lad smoke, he can push that window up there open a bit and lean out.'

'As long as no one minds.'

Everyone nodded at him to go ahead.

'Anyone else want a smoke?'

'I've never smoked in my life son, not about to start now.'

'It's good for pain you know, it could help,' said the lad pointing to her hands as he jumped up on to his chair.

The old woman looked down, she'd taken her gloves off and was rubbing her gnarled fingers.

'Aye, arthritis son, the pain gets worse when it's cold.'

'Am tellin you, smoke some of this and you'll no feel the pain any more,' he said opening the window, shivering as the cold wove its way in past him.

'I'm good thanks son, I wouldn't know how to smoke it even if I wanted to.'

'Marjory Pratt at Number 87, she'd definitely be top of my hit list,' the voice behind the desk announced.

'What's up with Marjory Pratt?'

'She's a nosy old busy body is what, in everyone's business, curtains twitching all hours, day and night. She's got it coming to her. It was all her fault my Nancy left me.'

'Nancy yer wife?'

'Aye, well she was, ran off with her college professor, I knew her going back to study was a bad idea.'

'So how's that got anything to do with the old busy body?'

'Well, the college professor's her son.'

'Ah!'

'That's better,' said the young lad, closing the window, restoring a smidge of warmth to the room along with a faint illicit scent.

The old woman put her gloves back on and glanced at each of us.

'I might have killed someone too,' she announced in what was barely a whisper.

She had everyone's attention.

'But it was a long time ago. Long, long time ago.'

'My Frank was a bully, a horrid bully, he deserved what he had coming to him.'

I was beginning to wonder if I should have just stayed in bed.

'I haven't thought about Frank in years. There was a few sleepless months, I tell you, when I saw our old house go back on the market, but thankfully they seemed to like the garden.'

The young lad looked shocked. 'Anyone else got anything they'd like to confess?' he asked.

'It was actually four boxes!' came the voice from behind

the desk.

'Maybe I'll try one of those cigarette thingies son, if you can you show me how to smoke it.'

As she stood and made her way over to the young lad, the old man turned to look at me.

'You've been awfy quiet son, what you got to say fur yersel?'

'DI Willis,' I said, 'It's a pleasure to meet you all.'

The Disappearing Act
by Abigail Johnson

Shortlisted for the Edinburgh Award for Flash Fiction 2021

"Uri Geller' I think he said. Words softer than the flutter of butterfly wings, the effort contorting his face. My dad had a thing about magic. I hold his hand and watch machines bleeping and blinking like satellites, measuring the fading hum of breath and heartbeat. A nurse checks his pulse, unaware we're both strangers to him.

'Not long now,' she nods, as my stomach folds in on itself, a knot I know I'll never untangle.

The last time I saw him, I was seven. He pulled a coin from behind my ear and later guessed the number I was thinking of. I had no idea when he'd next turn up, appearing from nowhere like a rabbit from a hat.

And now, for his grand finale, he's about to disappear for good.

In suffocating silence, I hover at his bedside. 'I'm a cardiologist, Dad. Married, three kids. I went to Oxford University. I travel a lot, speaking at conferences all over and …'

I don't tell him how I'd sit by the window every birthday, hoping it would be the year he'd come back. Even though I want him to know.

Afterwards, I tell my friend Jay about Dad's last words.

'What, the spoon guy?'

'Yep,' I said. 'I know he liked magic and everything, but still. His last words to me?'

'Are you sure he didn't say, *'you're incredible?*''

I play with the words silently. And just like that, the line between love and hate is blurred. His final trick.

Egg
by Eleanor Thom

Longlisted, Scottish Arts Club Short Story Competition 2021

Six weeks after Ruthie was born, Dora was back in the kitchens and all through November she secretly cried into the boiling pans. But people were good to her, even when she was distracted, even when she dropped a bowl of soup into a gentleman's lap. She still carries the sadness inside, but now that her milk has dried up, she has quietened down.

There are plenty eggs for the elderly residents, so Cook always spares Dora one. Since Passover this has been a Friday ritual. Dora takes off her hat and uncrosses the straps of her apron. Her uniform is bundled into the laundry with the other whites and Dora says goodbye to Cook.

"Gut Shabbes, Dora. Don't forget Ruthie's egg!"

Dora takes her usual route down Oranienburgerstrasse, cupping the egg close to her chest. The crowd nudges along, glad for the weekend, struggling with the heat. There is not a breeze. Flags hang limp from their poles. Dora follows the raised railway along Dircksenstrasse. A train rumbles overhead and she imagines the egg yolk trembling inside the shell. By the time she reaches Alexanderplatz it is warm in her hand. Here the buses, trams and trains loop in and about each other but they somehow disentangle themselves to follow their own routes out of the busy square.

Home. She cooks the egg as soon as she gets in. Tip-tap. Tip-tap. The egg has a bright, pale shell. Dora simmers it with her fingertips on the handle of the pan, watching the bubbles form in the water. At domestic school they taught her the surest way to protect the egg from cracking: a spoonful of salt in the pan.

Her cousin is not home yet. Perhaps she is staying out,

taking time to be alone with Herbert. When they come in, they will bring noise, Meta's chirpy stories, Herbert's whistling, the smell of his cigarette. They never change.

Tip-tap. Tip-tap. Sweat is slick on her face as she stands over the pan. Dora is surprised she has any sweat left. Fridays are the busiest day at work. Pots are set to stew overnight and preparation is made for dinner. Three meals at once. It's like a king's feast every week. The egg spins in the black pan like a moon. As usual Dora has forgotten to time the cooking. Three minutes is all it takes to get lost in her thoughts. She will let it simmer longer.

According to the dietary laws you have fleischig and milchig, and eggs are neither. This has always puzzled Dora. They taste more like dairy, but they come from flesh and could be flesh again. Laid by a kosher hen, they are pareve and can be eaten with meat or with dairy. Not that it matters to Dora. She would eat anything at all.

Cook tries her best to nourish the residents with alternatives since the kosher ban. She stocks cheeses, nuts, eggs and milk, but the elderly are stuck in their ways and some of them grumble and pick at their plates. Dora misses the ones who were livelier once, who are irritable now, no longer laughing.

Cook still makes a kind of cholent for Saturday, following as closely as she can the old recipe, just without the meat. She throws the ingredients into the pots as big as barrels: potatoes, beans, paprika, onions and barley. Just before sundown a whole basketful of eggs is placed gently into the mixture, left in their shells to slowly bake and by Saturday afternoon the onions will have dyed the eggshells a deep russet red. The dyed shells remind everyone of Pesach: the egg on their plate a symbol of how hard life was. And because of the deep ruby shells they also think of Easter, when the Germans paint their Paschal eggs. Easter and Passover. In Spring, eggs are on the Seder plate and hanging in the trees.

Dora leaves the salted water to cool. She puts the egg in a cup on the table and from a drawer she takes out a pocket paint palette. On the palette she sees the dried swirls of colour she used the previous week. While Dora goes to wash, the egg waits on the table.

At first Ruthie was too young to eat the eggs Cook gave her. Dora made pinholes in each end of the shell and carefully blew into the hole at the top, emptying the insides into a bowl. She used the insides to make a treat for Meta's sweet tooth, eierkuchen with a spoon of sugar and flour, spreading it with a little jam if they had some.

The shells were painted for Ruthie. Dora had to make sure she didn't crush them as she rode the bumpy tram to Niederschönhausen. At the infant home the aunties tied a branch over Ruthie's cot and the eggs were threaded and hung there so the decorations spun and bounced. Each weekend, Ruthie's tree got a new jewel. But Ruthie is nine months old now and she has developed a good appetite. "Mutti brought you an egg!"

This is what Dora will say to Ruthie as she lifts her out of the cot, the moment she waits for all week.

Painting the egg helps time to pass. At first Dora found it difficult, but since Meta found a tiny paintbrush, Dora's decorating has been more precise.

"What a shame," Meta always says. "That is far too pretty to eat!" but Meta does not see Ruthie's face when the colourful egg appears from Dora's bag. She has not played the game of rolling the egg along the ground to crack the shell, or watched how Ruthie eats, smacking her lips, licking each fingertip, with crumbled yoke sticking to her chin.

Meta and Herbert are still not home. Meta used to wait for Herbert every day in a little park just south of the Spree. This is not allowed any more. Dora misses swimming in the baths behind the same park. Jews are not allowed there either. Tonight, the Lewins might be strolling by the river, or walking under the conker trees behind Unter den Linden. No one can stop them walking together. If only Marcus had been more like Herbert, Dora could have had someone to stroll beside her while she pushed Ruthie's pram.

Dora has just finished washing herself when the Lewins arrive home. "Post for you, Dora," Meta calls.

"Did you walk far?"

"No. It is too hot," Meta complains.

Meta will go and change out of her work clothes. While she does this Herbert will be making coffee and looking forward to smoking a cigarette. He will be hungry, already wondering what Dora is going to cook.

Dora wraps a towel around herself and tucks a corner of it under her arm.

Herbert greets her quickly and taking his coffee, follows Meta into their bedroom. Dora's clothes are kept in the corner of the kitchen, just above her bed. The letter is on the table.

Her name and address are neatly typed in heavy ink and the paper is bone-dry in the heat. She feels her chest tighten as she pushes a finger under the seal. There is a single sheet of paper inside and a black eagle stamp.

Dora reads a few words. Her skin is cool after washing, but she feels the heat dewy on her. Drips fall from her fringe. A drop lands with a tap on the words.

According to the police order of 22.08.1938 regarding Jewish aliens residing the territory of the Reich, you are ordered to leave within one month and may not return without permission.

You have a right to file a complaint within two weeks of this instruction which would have to be submitted in writing.

You will face imprisonment for one year and fines should you return to the Reich without permission.

Dora stares at the rough opening her fingers have slit through the envelope. The heat is growing in the room and in Dora's head. Meta finds her moments later and reads the letter.

"How can they do this?" Meta says. Her voice is thin, like someone being held round the neck. "You have not broken any laws."

Dora holds the torn envelope over her chest.

Herbert reads the letter too and she sees in his face that he can do nothing. He says they will think of something.

Herbert lights candles. Dora puts the food in front of them, but no one eats.

"Vati was not German," Dora blurts into the silence. "That is the reason. You didn't get letters, did you? Because your father is German and Herbert is German."

"If you were married to a German, it could change things," Herbert shrugs. "Maybe Marcus?"

The sudden sound of his name surprises her. She hasn't said his name in a year, not since Ruthie was born.

Meta snorts. "Marcus only does what his parents want." Herbert clears his plate noisily and goes to the window. "What is there to stay for anyway?" he says.

The window is open and outside neighbours are fighting over the rubbish bins.

Dora has never seen Herbert like this before. He goes out, slamming the door as if he is annoyed by her. Herbert would like to emigrate with Meta. They tried, but it was too expensive and they had no contacts. On top of this, Meta said she would never leave without her mother and that made it impossible.

Even more than emigrating, Meta and Herbert want a baby. They have been married three years and people have started talking. It is unfair. Even when Dora was carrying Ruthie, Meta seemed to feel more motherly than she did. Meta is more mamish than her in every way.

"I wish we could all leave," Dora says.

Her cousin hangs over her like a coat. She wraps her hands over Dora's fists and they cry as if they are trying to melt into one.

Dora can't still her hand to paint the egg. She was going to paint a ship, clouds swirling at the top, lilac and grey, a curl of yellow at the edges. The calm waves would ripple with a thousand tiny arcs.

Meta paints it for her. She cleans the brush with a swirling motion in the glass of water. It rings like a tiny bell. Every so often Meta gets to her feet and goes to the kitchen. She brings back clean water. Meta does this without a word till eventually the ship is sailing.

When Herbert returns, he squeezes a hand on Dora's shoulder. "I'm sorry, Dora," he says. "We will look after Ruthie. It's a promise."

Dora takes the letter with the eagle and the hakenkreuz and hides it in her bag. When she gets into bed, she wishes she could reach right over the city. She imagines the cot, the white blankets and Ruthie's tiny hands tucked below her chin. Most nights Dora can trick herself to sleep, but tonight it doesn't work. Ruthie feels far away.

She thinks about Vati. She wishes he were still here to offer some advice, even some prayers. Dora hasn't prayed in a long time. She doesn't even remember her Hebrew lessons. She is not a very good Jew and she is not a real German. She is as stateless a person as it's possible to be, she thinks. The same as the egg. Always puzzling, always between states, not quite dairy, not quite flesh, a mother, but not quite.

She has nothing left to do but pray.

Dora's thoughts blend like the paint in the water. She feels seasick and she wonders how it is possible. She has never even seen the sea.

For my grandmother, Deborah Wilson née Tannenbaum (1916-1980)
Ruth Rosa Tannenbaum (1937-1943)
Meta Lewin née Rowelski (1912-1943)
Herbert Oswald Lewin (1910-1943)

Remember
by Margaret Callaghan

Shortlisted for the Edinburgh Award for Flash Fiction 2021

I see you sometimes. A shape at the window, rags and bones crossing the street. I helped you up when you fell once. Did you find your glasses in your pocket? Did you know it was me?

I hear you sometimes. I come to your flat and listen at the door. You still sing well, though you said the band had wanted you for your looks. One time you'd broken the lock. You were passed out on couch. I switched off the oven, cleaned the beans from the wall, laid a blanket over you. Did you know someone was there? Did you hope it was me?

Do you remember the caravan holiday? We had pineapple cakes for breakfast and went swimming in the rain. You left me in the playpark while you went for one drink. It was dark when you came back. I was sitting on the swings, reading by the sodium lights.

You used to bring my coat to school when it rained. My teacher always giggled when she saw you. She said it was hard to believe you were my dad.

Do you remember racing me down the hill to the library? Your stories were better than books. Sometimes I'd fall asleep reading and you'd slide my glasses off gently. But I knew you were there.

Do you wish you hadn't stormed out of my graduation, fallen through a hedge at my wedding, slept through her funeral?

I see you sometimes. Do you see me?

Pica
by Jupiter Jones

Longlisted, Scottish Arts Club Short Story Competition 2021

All our friends had cautioned against optimism. But after only two attempts at impregnation, with my feet up on the blue ottoman and the sound of Thelonious Monk drifting up the spiral staircase, our offspring was conceived and I began to grow, 'Vaster than empires and more slow', like Marvell's marvellous vegetable love. Everything was perfect. I was to be Ma and my wife, Celine, would be Pa.

In the beginning, I was sick, then not so sick, then I craved yoghurt. Then I went off yoghurt and wanted salt.

'Lay off the salt,' said Celine. 'Think of your blood pressure.'

I ate anchovies. Tin after tin after tin. Celine went to the cash-and-carry for them and I peeled back the fiddly ring-pull lids and picked them out in my fingers. With my head tipped back, eyes closed in ecstasy, like the ecstasy of the Magdalene, I dropped the little fish, slick with oil, one by one, into my greedy mouth. Sometimes I swallowed them whole and their slippery salty bodies and little bones like whiskers slid down my throat. I was a gannet.

'Rather you than me, babe,' said Celine as she watched me gorge myself.

Pica, they said at the ante-natal clinic. Unusual craving. But not really pica, not the clinically very mad kind, like wanting to eat hair, or metal, or chalk-dust. Just a curious side effect of pregnancy; an appetite temporarily out of kilter.

Other things were out of kilter. My senses of taste, smell and humour were different. My skin and my patience were stretched thin. External horizons narrowed as my inside-self expanded and became dominant – as if I was thinking with my belly. Celine was solicitous, she did her best, but *we* were out of kilter.

I told her about pica.

'There was a girl at school ate hair,' she said. 'She was proper weird and very good at maths. They took her away eventually.'

'Because she was gifted?'

'No dummy. Because she had hair-balls blocking her intestines.'

This, or maybe the pica gave me nightmares. Night after night I dreamed of anchovies. At first, they were like synchronized swimmers choreographed by Busby Berkeley around our unborn offspring. They swished and rippled and shimmied, swirling arcs and circles of flashing silver and electric blue. They made figures-of-eight and stars and Catherine wheels. A kaleidoscope of dancing fish patterns evolving and dissolving with every twist. Then, like maypole dancers, they began to weave their pattern more tightly, lacing concentric circles. Swimming in and swimming in until they were a writhing bolus of fish converging feverishly, devouring our baby with pointed little teeth. I woke with cramps. My belly packed tight with excitable anchovies, the pain was intense: an indigestible knot of fear and fish.

When I described all this, Celine laughed. Her paternal great-grandmother, Hester, was famous, she said, for eating coal during all ten of her pregnancies.

'They say she'd sit in the coal shed, hands black, lips black, sometimes she'd put pieces of coal in her skirt pockets, sneaking it out to lick, even in church, and always ratted-out by tell-tale black stains on her lips. But who has coal nowadays?'

'Did she dream?'

Celine shrugged and turned down the under-floor heating; it was spring after all.

'Cut back on the bloody anchovies. It's probably just indigestion,' she said.

She was probably right. Because of the vivid dreams, I was afraid to eat the anchovies, but somehow, without meaning to, I ate them anyway. I would wake in the early hours with dreams and cramps and I'd weep and foreswear all fish. But later, during the ordinariness of daytime, the fear wore off and, by noon, the insatiable desire returned and easily overcame my resolve. Unexpectedly, I would find I had a tin in my hand, a fish in my mouth, oil down my chin. Then, as dusk deepened, I'd become increasingly anxious and ashamed of my lack of will-power. Like Hester, I ate in secret, crouching out of sight, gulping them down behind closed doors, hiding empty tins in next-door's rubbish. It felt creaturely, less than human. Celine knew. When she kissed me, surely, she could taste them on my breath? Was it like kissing a seabird, a pelican?

'Booby,' she said, but bought more tins without further comment.

Perhaps because of the fish dancing in my belly I was tired and began napping in the afternoons. Then it was easier to stay awake much of the night, avoiding the salty dreams. I roamed the house, read poetry, Marvell of course, and Byron, particularly *Childe Harold's Pilgrimage*, and watched old black and white films with the sound turned off. One night, there was a thunderstorm. Celine slept through it, curled warm in our bed like a slender question mark. Wrapped in a blanket, perched on the window seat looking out over the garden, I watched the trees, whipped and howling in fear and protest. I watched the dark wet sky splitting open again and again. By dawn, our gutters were blocked with twigs and leaves, still green, detached too early, and the fence was down.

That was how we first met Frank. Celine got out ladders and cleared the gutters, but she rang Handy Frank about the fence. He said he was busy, mad-busy, but could fit us in before the weekend. Friday morning, we were having breakfast when his van pulled up outside. Frank was short and muscly with dyed black hair and little gold hoop earrings.

'A pirate, a land-locked pirate,' Celine said dismissively.

After he fixed the fence, he mended the gate, and then he agreed to build some decking for us. We imagined long late summer evenings and ice-cold gin cocktails.

Frank eyed me up and down with reverence, as one might gaze at the Madonna.

'I know this is probably weird,' he said, 'but could I feel your belly? Would you mind?'

I said no, that is no, I wouldn't mind. But I lied. His hands disturbed me and *Childe Harold* lay silent under Frank's fingers.

I said to Celine that I wanted to delay the installation of the decking.

'Why so?'

'Just for a while, until I am delivered.'

'But then we'd have missed the best of the summer.'

'Does it have to be Frank?

'Well, yeah, why not?'

'I thought he was a pirate?'

She laughed, 'Oh I'm sure he is. A brigand of the very worst sort.'

The builders' merchant delivered stacks of timber, Frank arrived with power tools and the air was thick with their buzz and drone. I preferred to stay upstairs, out of the way, but my afternoon sleeps were fitful. Celine was working from home that week, but she frequently strayed from her desk and spent time in the garden, drinking coffee with Frank. Restless with heartburn, I watched them from between the slats of venetian blinds, envying Celine with her lithe figure, her fluidity of movement, her faultless performance of insouciance. And begrudging the way Frank commandeered her attention as he measured and cut and smoothed the planks. I watched Celine, push her hair behind her elfin ears and hoot at Frank's long, convoluted and politically incorrect jokes. Snatches of conversation drifted in through the windows with the sweet scent of sawn iroko.

'Not long now till that baby is born.'

'No, not long. August.'

'So, two mothers?'

'Yes. Two.'

'But you are not really going to call the poor mite Childe Harold, are you?'

'Yes, Harold, Harry.'

'How did you two ladies decide which one of you would be pregnant?'

'We just knew.'

'Did you flip a coin?'

'No. We just knew.'

'And the father? The real father, I mean, the biological?'

Oh, the usual questions. So predictable. Frank seemed genuinely shocked that you could order paternity on the internet. Blonde, blue-eyed, very tall and academically gifted.

After Harold was born, blonde and blue-eyed, my body remained baggy and oversized. The tins of anchovies sat at the back of the cupboard. I had no desire for them. I couldn't even remember why I had wanted them so badly, why they had been so *necessary*. Now, my appetite was broad and indiscriminate, I put food, anything, whatever was to hand, in my mouth, without really thinking. I chewed and swallowed. I reached for more. Sleep came in snatches, brief and dreamless.

Baby Harold was asleep in his pram out on the decking and shaded from the Indian summer sun by a striped awning. Eating cheese triangles, I wandered barefoot into the study, where Celine was at her desk, hunched over, deep in concentration. She was designing a tree house to go in the big sycamore at the bottom of the garden. It was an elaborate thing on three levels with a crow's nest look-out, brise-soleil for shade, a trap door and a rope ladder.

'It will be a while before Harry is big enough to climb the ladder,' I said, leaning over her shoulder to see the plans and design catalogues spread over her desk.

'It's not really for him,' she said. 'Just something I've always kind of wanted. A hankering, you know?'

I dropped a kiss on her white-blonde head.

'I know. A castle in the air.'

'We could escape up there, drink cocktails, read poetry, listen to jazz, lounge about like lizards.'

'Escape?'

'You know.'

I did.

'Will Frank build it?' I asked.

'Well, I shall certainly give him a call, ask him to quote.'

I nodded.

After three months, I was still vast. Baby-weight girdled me like a flab-coloured stab vest. Celine was encouraging; she bought digital bathroom scales and low-fat foods: wafer thin turkey-ham, crispbreads, non-stick spray, fatless spreads. And kale.

Every morning she weighed me and was disappointed.

'Take up running,' she said.

She went online and ordered me some very expensive running shoes. Neon blue and silver, light as air. They fitted perfectly and, because she'd gone to such trouble, I felt I had no option, so I began to run in the park, sluggishly, usually at dusk, ashamed of my oscillating belly. If my growing had been slow, my ungrowing was at the pace of a snail. Stepping onto the scales became awkward. Celine's

177

sympathy ebbed.

'I just don't see,' she said, 'why, with the low-fat food and the running, that you're not getting any thinner.'

But having no willpower, I snacked like a motherfucker. Chorizo, peanut butter, biscuits, scotch eggs, malt loaf, taleggio, spicy chicken wings, hunks of brioche dipped in chimichurri or marmalade.

Eventually, Celine said, 'Think of it like this. You want to lose a stone, that's fourteen pounds. Think of it as blocks of lard.'

I thought about it. I thought about solid white fat, I thought about my girdle of blubber. I wondered if by eating anchovies I had become a whale and I twisted to look over my shoulder for a tail that wasn't there, but despite all the thinking, I couldn't *think* myself thin. So, Celine made it real. She went shopping and came home with twenty-eight half-pound blocks of lard. She stacked them in the fridge. Not much room left for her low-fat spread, or my taleggio.

'Now when you go to the fridge for a snack, you'll see lard and stay strong.'

She was right. Of course she was right. I ate less, ran more, ran faster. The weight began to fall away.

This morning, I went running in the park. The trees were magical, their limbs silvered with the first hoar frost, lit by slanting shards of early light and I felt elated by endorphins dancing through my body. When I got home, I found Harry strapped into his baby-bouncer, red in the face, wailing furiously for attention. Celine, still in her blue silk pyjamas, was sitting on the kitchen floor, her legs spread wide, eyes glazed. Fingers smeared thickly with white fat. Her chin and lips slick with grease as she gorged herself on my lard.

Hungry Bird
by Alexander Hamilton

Longlisted for the Edinburgh Award for Flash Fiction 2021

Old woman had said that no soul had ever escaped the Crane and, when her time came, she wanted Boy to put a slab of clay over her heart.

The Crane was nearly at the door as he snatched up the last of the clay and daubed it on Old Woman, then he hid, cowering at the back of the hut. The Crane angled in through the doorway, stilting over to Old Woman. It looked at her corpse, cocking its head, bright deadly eyes seeking the souls hiding place, but though the shape was right the smell was wrong and it couldn't make out the timid soul twitching deep inside Old Woman. It gave a harsh cracking cry, cheated of its prey. It stared unblinkingly straight at Boy. With a huffle of its feathers it stalked out of the hut

Boy crept over to Old Woman who looked younger and happier than he had ever seen her. He sat on his heels beside Old Woman eating his rice cake, he was now alone. The desolation of his situation lay heavy on his heart and a tear welled and slowly traced the grime on his cheek. So absorbed was he, that he was quite unaware of the Crane, sharp legs bent, stepping Of course, towards him, head back, eyes beady bright, dagger beak poised.

The Crane, its ash white plumage streaked and spotted by more than the setting sun, slowly flapped over the marsh with something in its beak.

The Opportunist
by Frances Sloan

Longlisted, Scottish Arts Club Short Story Competition 2021

I hoped he would and he did. He told me to keep the change after putting two-pound coins on the counter. It's the least he could do. He'd wandered round and round this charity shop for at least twenty minutes, before buying a book. Now that he's gone, I pocket the coin. His contribution brings my total income today to six pounds and fifty-five pence.

The five fifty-five came from a flat clearance dumped here this morning. There were bags and bags of unwashed clothes and sheets, none of it was even fit for recycling. The clothes belonged to a man of my build. You wonder has he died or is he lying on a pavement somewhere? It disturbed me when I pulled out a checked shirt, same as my own. I had a fleeting vision of myself as that man. But going by the smell, I'm guessing that the shirt owner is, or was, a big drinker and that's not my thing. My reward for gagging through the stench from those bags was some loose change in the bottom of a shoe box.

I've learnt that donated clothes, in particular, can be an unexpected source of forgotten cash. Right now, I'm observing one of our regulars, who also realises a pocket's potential. With a deft hand, he explores the jackets and jeans. He's wasting his time on my watch. My jackpot, to date, is fifty pounds, found in the side pocket of a dead man's jacket. A lady, I assumed to be his widow, had brought in boxes of folded clothes.

'I hope you can sell them,' she said. 'He never got to wear most of them.'

It was good stuff, designer gear. The poor man couldn't have been that old. I found the money a few minutes after she had left and hesitated just for a short while. The way I looked at it, he was dead. The money was better off with me, a living soul. I invested it in the bookies next door and my horse came in, 20:1. What a win!

I had placed my bet at lunchtime that afternoon. Later, after the race, I left the shop on the pretext of buying milk, returning a short time later, milk in hand and a wad of notes in my pocket.

It was the horse's name that appealed to me – Delia, rhymes with Celia: my ex-wife. It was hard to hide my elation. As a gesture to the dead man, I put ten pounds into the till. Kate, the manager, believed that I had found it in a donated jacket. I'm not a dishonest man, just an unemployed one who has taken risks now and again.

The risks were too much for Celia.

'I love you, Brian, but for Sam's sake you should go,' she said.

I left and, to be fair, I saw Sam as much as I wanted – for a while, anyway. Then innocent little Sam told her about his visit to Daddy's flat. She thought we were at the cinema watching *Jungle Book*.

'Enjoy the film, Sam?' she asked when I brought him home. 'Did you see lots of animals?'

'Just the gee-gees and Daddy's gee-gee won,' he announced as he jumped up and down.

'Can we do that again, Daddy?'

Had he not been so excited at my win, I might have continued to see Sam, but from then on Celia monitored my visits and outings with a sharp eye. I am now obliged to produce receipts from any trips to the cinema or McDonalds and give her a full account of our 'father-son' time together.

I handed her fifty pounds that day and she threw it at me. 'Dirty money' she called it and it must have been, as I lost it the next day on a horse called Spiced Up.

It's strange to stand here selling cast-off clothes, rather

than life insurance. To lose my job was bad enough, but worse still to lose my wife, my son and my home. It's true my redundancy money had disappeared a bit too soon online, but I was on a winning streak when Celia blocked our credit card. She reckoned I was an addict. I pointed out to her that, in my previous job, clients put money on their lives. They were the greatest gamblers of all.

I started volunteering here to please Celia.

'Please get help,' she had pleaded.

So, I related my problems to a doctor who advised me to do some voluntary work.

'Get out there,' he said; 'mingle with people.'

He had offered me antidepressants, but I refused them. The solution to my problems is obvious – money.

I have a theory about money and it all stems from a couple of Bible quotes.

"To those who have, more will be given ..."

Look around you at the 'haves' and 'have nots' for evidence of this. These days I'm one of the 'have nots'.

I try to keep a couple of pounds from my benefits for a lotto ticket and a scratch card. I've won as much as forty on a card, though not for a while. That's the other bit of that Bible quote.

"... but from those who have nothing, even what they have will be taken away."

I'm returning to an empty flat tonight, with six fifty-five to tide me over the weekend. I'm supposed to take Sam out tomorrow. At least the park is free.

It's quiet in the shop now. Friday afternoons often are and give me some peace to hunt through the stock for something worthwhile to pass to Jimmy, my bookie-buddy. He's about the only friend I have. My previous companions disappeared, deserting me when funds ran dry. Jimmy operates as a car-boot salesman every Saturday morning. We split the profits if he sells any of my finds.

182

I've found some shirts lying in the sorting area. They aren't even out of their packaging. Taking them is a bit of a risk, as I'm not sure if Kate noticed them yesterday. But I need some money. A quick text to Jimmy and we're in business.

The way I look at it, someone gave those shirts away. They didn't cost the shop anything and I deserve something for all the heavy work Kate asks me to do. She seems glad to have me, the only man about the shop. I sometimes think she fancies me. The other volunteers are all retired ladies, the sort I used to charm money from, in insurance sales.

I don't tell Kate about my bits and pieces of extra income. She just wouldn't understand. Last month she found eight hundred pounds in a lady's handbag and made it her mission to get the money back to its owner. She found the lady in a local nursing home. What a waste! The less money you have in those places, the better. That cash would have been better in my hands. Think of the profit if Delia had been racing.

I hope these two aren't bringing me more rubbish to sort.

'Afternoon. We've brought some money.' The woman is saying.

Her male counterpart carries two large plastic bags full of coins and deposits them beside me.

'We do this,' he's saying. 'Throw our loose change into glass jars for a year, then give it to a charity. It's your turn this year, but you've a bit of counting to do. We reckon there may be up to £200 there.'

My heart beats fast as I smile at them. I offer to take their address and forward a receipt after I count the money. They decline, saying they trust we'll put it to good use. Then they're gone.

If I work fast, I'll have the money counted and my share taken before Kate comes to lock up. I feel a little high seeing these piles of coins. It's about time I had a little luck and, for sure, they chose the right charity.

'How are you, Brian? How are we doing today?'

Damn it, it's Kate. I didn't expect her for another couple of hours.

'Not too many sales, Kate. I've been busy earlier with that flat clearance.'

'Anything of value?'

'Not a thing.'

'Those shirts behind you should sell well.'

'Should do – I was about to price them when these bags of cash arrived.'

'Wow!' she says. 'Where did these come from?'

I explain about the jar emptying couple and cannot suppress a deep sigh.

'You may as well go on Brian,' she's saying, 'you seem tired. I'll bag these coins.'

I feel sick, not tired, but I give up for today. Jacket on and I'm off home. My hand hits against something in my right pocket and I remember the donation.

This puts me in a bit of a dilemma. I should tell Kate about the young man who came into the shop earlier – a hoodie. I observed him while he looked at trainers and football tops. He stood in the same place for what seemed like a long time. I was about to suggest he leave when he came up very close to me. So close, he scared me.

'I want to give money to the refugees,' he said. 'Would your charity send it through for me?'

'Sure,' I replied. 'I'll hand it over to our manager when she comes in.'

He gave me fifty pounds, then ran out the door before I could even acknowledge his generosity. My hand is holding tight to that cash right now. To siphon off a few coins earlier would have been fine, but can I take money meant for refugees?

Though – am I not a refugee? Forced to leave my home. I

184

could borrow this money. Yes, borrow. Invest it again in the bookies and once I make a profit, give some of it to refugees or indeed to any needy people.

Jimmy just texted me a good tip on a horse.

'A dead cert,' he's saying.

I need a break. But a dead cert with this money. And what if the young hoodie comes back?

Maybe I'll just invest twenty-five on the horse and declare twenty-five to Kate. But I'd regret that if the horse wins. She isn't looking. I'll toss this coin for it. Heads I keep the money, tails I hand it to Kate.

Then again, maybe best out of three?

A Story on a Postcard
by Peter Watson

Shortlisted for the Edinburgh Award for Flash Fiction 2021

Dad wouldn't go away on holiday,
so Mum took her holidays by herself
in the small seaside town where she lived.
Each morning,
she left him at home
and went out on little excursions.
She took long walks on the beach,
she lunched in nice restaurants,
she went to the cinema,
she sent postcards to family and friends.
When Dad died,
she gave up taking her holidays at home.
She went to Paris!

The Picture on the Wall
by Frank Carter

Longlisted, Scottish Arts Club Short Story Competition 2021

M y, but it's quiet in here. *Seems there's just me and the picture up there on the wall.* I can hear myself think in here. I can feel my thoughts. Like little fishes they are, come tripping up to the surface and lots of little bubbles pop out. They are mine they are, them little fishes and the bubbles, my thoughts.

Now if you were daft enough to ask him, my George, about pictures and Art Galleries, he'd rip yer head off he would. 'Them places,' he says, 'them's for poofters – waste of tax payers' 'ard-earned cash.'

So when I thought I need a bit of peace to clear my head, I thought: where would George least like me to go to think? So here I am in Leeds to give myself a chance to get my thoughts straight.

Now I know you're thinking Leeds isn't going to give me peace and quiet but our Sally came here on a day out from school last year, did the university visit she did. Not that I know what she did but he asked her did she do Elland Road? And Sal said: 'No, we did the university.' And George huffed and puffed: 'Huh! waste of bleeding money.'

And they did dinner in Leeds too, only they called it lunch on account of them being there with Mr Shakespeare; he's their English teacher. And George wanted to know: 'Who's Mister Shakespeare when he's at home?'

'Chap who wrote plays in Elizabethan times,' says Sal.

'Oh,' said George.

Anyroads, in the afternoon they go to the Art Gallery. And that's where I am now.

I went to see my mum again yesterday. I don't think she's

got long now. My mum's one of my little fishes, keeps popping up with something to get me thinking. 'Your George,' she says, 'is just like your father. It's taken me until now to realise, but now I'm seeing things as they really are ... the man I married is a bully, always has been all our married life. The man YOU married, Christine, is a bully. Chris love, you know he is. But don't you be like me – like I am now. They've told me I've only got weeks – weeks! Don't be like me now, Christine!'

Don't know what I'll do without my mum. When I talk who'll listen? My mum could have painted the picture on the wall. She knows me better than anyone. It's not a picture of someone, is it? More a ... *a representation of something.*

See, there's a figure and it's muscular but I'm sure it's female, she has my buttocks and her raised arm hides my face – and my intentions. There's a shadow behind her, isn't there? Stooping, self-satisfied, set in his ways, controlling. I'll bet he doesn't know that the raised arm with all her power is raised at him!

I do love George. I hate George. I need George. Do I need George? He is my shadow; he follows my every move. He is the outside of my inside. People see my shadow and don't see me.

Physically, we have been apart for as long as I remember. He doesn't hold my hand, kiss my lips, stroke my back, fondle my hair. But he does want his marital rights he says! Ugh! And that's what he gets – for his manly pride or maybe out of duty to me but not for any reason that matters. Once a week – Thursday – bed – light off. I like to be touched. I want to be touched lovingly. And do I touch him? I do with my obedience, with my roast beef and my apple pie. But lovingly?

My mum asked me once: 'Did we not love you enough, Christine?' And she reminded me: 'We did have poor Joe to care for; he needed the lion's share; he was in his wheelchair while you were fine and fit. He needed your dad and me

188

more than you did. And the others, I needed you to help with the others, Christine. And Dad needed you to help me.'

So I was glad when I was wanted. I took George and his fumbling in the dark and his Victorian attitudes and his Catholic guilt. Took him as a promise of things to come. And there have been good times. I have a husband who never misses a day's work, who's given me two wonderful kids and let me get on with the job of bringing them up .... Let me get on, so long as I don't question George and his 'homely routines and simple pleasures' (says he). Good Heavens! he does go on: 'Where's me tea for little me? ... These veg from Carneys? ... This meat from Bob Lamb's?' ... always followed by ... 'best butcher meat in all of England'. Every summer holiday is a case of: 'You can book Drakesmere Farm for t' summer fortnight. Take tha' wet wear. Never rains but pours, down Drakesmere.' Oh dear.

I have never complained because I have never actually felt discontented. I have been happy with the same old routine really. Am I ungrateful, am I taking a risk now when I suggest there has to be more than dreary days and lonely nights? Isn't there more to life?

Not just me that's affected either. Our Andrew cannot get even a word or a look from his father since the lad hit him with the revelation of his sexuality. I am not surprised and indeed welcome the news, since it explains to me a lot about my son. I smile and hold Andrew tight and smell his breath and love him all the more at this minute. But I am hardly prepared for George's onslaught and readiness to 'beat the devil' out of the boy. 'I am not having any son of mine ... I bring the boy up decent and what thanks do I get ... I blame you for namby-pambying him ... I this ... I that ... I ... I ...'

He's twenty-two and old enough to know what he is and what he isn't. Listen to him, George. Listen to yourself, George ... Andrew deserves this from his mother at the very least. But now he has to live away from home ... until he sees sense, George says … or until his mother does.

The picture again. The shadow in the picture does not listen. Just lurks and watches and passes judgements. Whatever you do, whatever you think, whatever you feel, the shadow knows.

My mother dying in hospital, my father going about his usual business, his only worry is where his next meal is coming from. Mum has lived for him and done for him. Cared for all of us – well, up to a point – and if Joe did have the lion's share, Dad commandeered what was left. George? Did I choose George to be a father to me – to be my kind of father?

Sally's view is very different. She declares herself opposed to marriage, pointedly telling her dad and me that too often marriage enslaves the woman in a dysfunctional lifestyle.

Dysfunctional! Oh George – he erupts but only because he catches the tone of what she is saying; he has no interest in what 'dysfunctional' might mean. Sal doesn't let the subject drop; she says I'm a slave to him – as if I didn't know. Her dad has already switched off, blaming a university education for his daughter's downfall from his high moral standards. My fault again – for encouraging her to go to university in the first place. I reap what I sow, he likes to tell me …. repeatedly.

Mother! I love Sal lecturing me as 'mother'! Mother, you are an intelligent woman (I protest), you should be out living your own life – no listen! – you can be a perfectly good wife and mother and still be YOU. I'm so feeble. Sally says what I say quietly to myself. She speaks out, voluble, confident. The picture is assertive.

I am … at a crossroads.

Mr Stanley Richardson enters the Alliance and Leicester Building Society. His arrival is a grand event. The American gentleman, we call him. He calls here after his lunch in town on the last Thursday of every other month. I notice and count on his coming, for it is always my desk he comes to. I handle his account and have done for ten years now. He is my Knight in Shining Armour, or so the girls say, and he greets me SO respectfully, smiles just at me SO … sensually … thanks me SO sincerely … Mr Richardson. Oh, Mr Stanley Richardson, were I Mrs Stanley Richardson …!

The colours are strong and forceful. Streaks of blood red – an angry red. And the background is blue … everywhere blue.

It is OK to dream a little, surely? So what am I? Driven? I need to be strong and I need to please. I do struggle to stand back and take stock and make decisions for ME. It seems I play the same old record over and over. The needle sticks – me too. I am like my mum, compelled to keep things the same – even if that means we get hurt. What do I really want from this life? I am 45 years of age and what do I dream of? Mr Richardson? Andrew at peace with himself? Sally opening new doors for her and for me? Mum not to suffer any more? Dad just to go away? And George to go with him! But do I dream for ME?

The picture on the wall has become demanding … overwhelming … Did I paint it myself?

No!

Oh! I peep round. Did anyone register that that 'no' came from me? Yet, I can leave the gallery with renewed hope and conviction. My time has come.

The train back from Leeds runs to time and I find myself contemplating my next move with a sense of …. exhilaration. Like a child off to a party. I know there are one or two things to see to first: George has a Darts match tonight; he'll need his green club shirt … and they'll want sandwiches …

Dr Anderson is an unpleasant surprise when I arrive home. And all my little fishes are suddenly nowhere. I just gawp at him and he takes my hand.

'Now, sit down, Mrs Ackroyd, there's nothing to worry about. George has had a slight stroke ... he's asleep at the moment ... been overdoing it. He's best not disturbed at all. Just try to keep things as they are ...'

The Concert
by Ann Seed

Shortlisted for the Edinburgh Award for Flash Fiction 2021

His paper cup, now weighted with my two-pound coins, sat more comfortably on the dog-peed cobbles.

"How you doing?" I asked.

"Would you like a song?" he replied.

He reached for his guitar, propped weathered and worn against the wall. His assuredness was at odds with his eyes. They were pale, floating in alcohol ... drugs ... maybe both ... They spoke of lostness, abandonment. When hardship had drowned him. But he smiled. His guitar was perfectly in tune, like his voice. He sang softly, living the music dug deep where the poison couldn't reach. Did he once have lessons? A warm bed, kisses goodnight?

He looked right at me, weaving with his words a world we shared for passing minutes, immune from the brokenness.

The lane had long settled, like an old man deep in his armchair, happy to let the world drift by. But he was young, ages with my son. Sitting ragged on weeds. Handsomeness still lay on his face. Untangle the hair, feed him square meals ... he could be striding to a theatre, reaping applause, a living, for his talent. I clapped, held his eyes, yearned for him to belong, to have a mother.

I gave him a five-pound note, small price for a concert, and begged him to buy a coffee, a sandwich. I walked away in the sun-setting evening, turned, waved. He smiled, leant back against the wall.

Please ... *please* ... let him be loved by someone somewhere ... someone who misses him.

Hidden
by David Butler

Longlisted, Scottish Arts Club Short Story Competition 2021

Impassive, he watched the garda car turn in by the For Sale sign and trundle up the laneway. Just herself coming for him, by the looks of it. The car edged round the overgrown harrow, turned a slow circle about the yard as though reluctant to stop.

He laid the haft of the axe against the shed, watched her climb out of the driver's seat. Hatless, hair drawn back in an auburn ponytail too young for the uniform. 'Chopping logs, Marty?'

By way of an answer, he scratched at his stubble. Then, when her grey eyes declined to look away, he nodded, 'You're looking well.' She was. A few pound heavier, maybe. But she carried it. The collie had waddled arthritically over to her, tail revolving stiffly as a stick stirring paint. 'Hey, girl!' She hunkered down, let the bitch nose the back of her hand. 'I'd say you miss herself about the place.'

'You talking to me or the dog?'

'Both,' she squinted into the watery sunlight, playful, a trick she had of old. 'How's your mam getting on inside in the home? Has she settled in alright?'

'You haven't been in to see her.'

'No.' She broke eye contact, looked out over the waterlogged field. 'Any offers on the place?'

'None you might call serious.'

'Give it time.' She stood up straight. 'Can I've a word, Marty, d'you mind?'

He snorted, hacked a gob of phlegm down beside the axe-head, lifted his own head defiantly.

'I expect you know what's brought me out.'

'Maybe you'll tell me, Sergeant, and not have us playing at guessing games.'

'Will we go inside?'

'I'd as soon we stay out here.' He'd be damned if he'd let Clodagh Ledwidge play him like a rookie. He'd been sweet on her once. He'd be damned if he was about to let her play that card again.

'Whatever you say,' she shrugged.

'Well? I've about a dozen jobs I could be getting on with.'

She allowed her features take on a more official cast. 'You heard there's three lads lying in the ICU up in St Dymphna's since Sunday night?'

He scratched at his ear by way of reply.

'Three Dublin lads. Left for dead they were.'

'Sure that's common knowledge.' Without any hurry, he set about tossing the chopped logs singly and messily into the shed.

'You've nothing to say to me on the subject? It'd be off the record, mind.' She tucked a mutinous strand of hair behind her ear. 'Anything you tell me out here is strictly off the record, OK?'

'A courtesy visit?'

'If you like.'

'Then what I have to say is,' he straightened, wiped his palms on his jeans, 'it's a pity about them.'

'There's one of them young lads took a shotgun blast to the face. Caught him across here it did.'

'Yeah?'

'Word is, he might never see again.'

He took a moment before replying. 'That's a tough break.'

She shook her head, her lips a thin white line. Judgemental. That was one of the words his mother had always used about Clodagh Ledwidge. *She's judgemental, that one. And she has your head that turned, you can't see up from down. You want to wise up, Marty, she's stringing you along, is*

195

all. And hadn't she been right?

'Is that all you have to say to me, Martin?'

'The way I heard it, it was a blast of his own shotgun done that to him. A sawed-off shotgun.'

'And what else have you heard?'

'Ok,' he said. He wasn't about to be bested, not on his mother's place. His own place, for now. 'Three fine bucks down on a jaunt from Dublin, is what I heard. Out for a bit of craic.' His sarcasm hadn't come off. 'Looking to terrorise pensioners living out on their own, rob whatever little they keep about the place. Just like they done up in Denny Carroll's there last Sunday week.' He stared hard at her, daring her to look away. 'Just like they done to that couple out in Bagenalstown and he bedbound. Intensive Care, is it? Good enough for the cunts, is what I heard.'

She was looking at him now the way she used to. Clever. Quizzical. It had him on his guard. 'I can understand how you must feel.'

'Can you, now?'

'After what happened to your mother.'

'You don't know the half of it.' He wasn't going to allow this. He wasn't going to venture back into the past, not on Clodagh Ledwidge's terms. Not back to that night of all nights. The very night he'd sat in his car outside her place, hour after hour, suspicion eating him. She'd never come home.

The same night, though he'd never let on, that he'd found out his mother had Clodagh Ledwidge's mark all along.

Had she even winced, mentioning it? 'You don't know the half of what happened,' he repeated. 'No-one does.'

'Alright. So, tell me.'

He hesitated, weighed the possibility she was playing games with him. 'The ole fella's life insurance money. That's what they got away with that night, every last red cent of it. You see, she was the kind of silly ould woman kept it hidden

196

up in the hayloft there, stuck in the back of a battered ould trunk.'

She was surprised, he could see it.

'Only, she was too ashamed to admit it to anyone, after. Too ... *ashamed*.' Uninvited, a sob bubbled through his bitterness. 'Know what they done, to make her talk? Will I tell you?' He tried out a grin that hardened at once into a grimace. 'They trussed her up in a kitchen chair with a length of clothesline. Then they brought in the big pot she'd use at Christmas to scald the ham. As if they knew all along where it was hanging. They filled it to the brim, set it on the stove in front of her and brung it to the boil, all the time whispering into her ear how once it was scalding hot, they were going to tip it over her head.'

In his pocket the phone winced and pinged. He ignored it, but saw how it distracted her, how it drew her attention. His voice grew rough-edged. 'When it was bubbling away good-oh, one of my brave buckos grabbed her right hand,' he held up his own, examined it, 'and he would've thrust it into the water there and then if she hadn't of told them. Sixteen thousand euro. Sixteen. Cash. That's what they cleared out with.' He dared her to disbelieve. 'And even that wasn't the worst of what they took. Oh by God it wasn't. They took her independence. After that, she was never easy staying on out here. Even after I moved back out.' She appeared to be processing this new information. 'My *mother*.' He swallowed hard. 'You knew her, fuck's sake. How proud she was. How contrary. Wild horses wouldn't have dragged her into any ... *care* home.'

He knew what was coming next. He could've scripted it. He didn't let her take his hands. 'So if that's what's lying up in Dymphna's ICU with the shite bet out of them the way they won't forget it any time soon, I'd say good enough for the cunts.'

'Look. Martin. What happened to your mother ...?'

'I know what you're gonna say, so don't bother.' He'd put his fingers alongside her cheek. He couldn't have explained why he'd done that. What impulse. So the voice he put on had mockery in it. *'That was terrible, tsst, what they done to your old dear. Terrible! But it was over a year ago, like. Who's to say it was the same gang of lads at all?* And maybe you'd be right. But you tell me, Sergeant. What does three Dublin lads be doing driving around the backroads of Carlow in black night with a sawed-off shotgun?' Looking at her, her clear grey eyes, all the fight went out of him. 'What brought you out here, Clodagh? You come to arrest me, is it?'

'I'm not here to arrest anyone.'

'No?'

'Listen to me, Marty. Please. If it *was* you ...'

'If it was me. Go on.'

'If it was you and whoever else, it'll go far easier on you if you come clean.'

'That's what you came to tell me? Off the record, like?'

'Marty ...'

'I never once said it was me, don't forget that. All the same, I can't say I've any sympathy for them city fuckers. If that's a crime,' theatrically, he thrust out his wrists, 'you better take me in right now.'

'I came out to warn you. For your own sake. Those lads took one hell of a beating. Hurleys, was it? They were brought in unconscious, all three of them. There could be brain trauma, it's too early to say. The guards can't just let that go.'

Over her head, he allowed his gaze follow a cartwheel of crows.

'But if you were to go in, now. Off your own bat. Explain to them what those lads were up to. What you thought you were planning on doing...' Her hand was on his forearm. He looked at it until she took it away. 'It'd go a lot easier on you, is what I'm saying.'

'And the buck that's blinded?'

'If, like you say, it was his own shotgun … If there was a struggle over it …'

'Wouldn't know, Sarge.' He stooped for a log. 'You'll have to ask someone was there.'

Her lips were again the thin white line. 'Listen to me, Martin. They can't just ignore this. Let it go, like. Scangers or not, there'll be all kinds of pressure, with this an election year. You need to be smart about this.'

'Smart.'

'Their SUV. It was an ambush, that much is obvious. The whole thing was planned, start to finish.'

'Well? If it was?'

'Well if it was, there'll be phone-calls made. Messages. I dunno, a WhatsApp group set up. You think it's enough to delete messages? Martin, there'll be an entire trail of breadcrumbs, like. None of that stuff stays hidden anymore.'

'I stand warned.'

'Something like this,' her eyes had teared up, 'it's not going to stay hidden.'

What *wasn't* she telling him? Did they already know more than she was letting on? Hearing the catch in her voice, he coarsened. 'What I don't get, if the guards are so good at tracking people down, I mean, if you guys are so on the ball, how come you're never around when them bastards is terrorising old folk? Can you answer me that?'

She stood back, turned her back on him as though she didn't want him to read her emotions.

'Where were you the night my mother was terrified out of her wits?'

'Ok, Marty.' Her back still to him, she made for the car. The old collie followed her over, but she pushed it away. 'Ok.'

'Where were you, Clodagh?' he said, low enough now that she mightn't have heard it. He watched the car exit the yard, skirt the rusted harrow and trundle away down the laneway. When it had turned onto the road, he ruffled the old collie's neck. 'Where were you, Clodagh Ledwidge, hunh?'

He tossed the last of the logs into the shed. Then he fished out his phone. He weighed it. Be smart, she'd said.

After some minutes he opened up the WhatsApp group. There was a lone interrogation mark. A scythe. A reaping hook. He'd be smart alright. Time enough to 'Clear Chat', after. Time enough. With a calloused thumb, he began to tap out a message.

Cheating
by Joanna Miller

Longlisted for the Edinburgh Award for Flash Fiction 2021

He stalks me. Persistent, patient. Thinking the time will be of his choosing.

Yesterday he caught me on Big Moor, sweeping me back to Argyll, to the wild deer and the fox on the winding single track road.

He is a thief. Exchanging love and happiness for loss and grieving.

I could make a diamond from your ashes, scatter them to the wind and the roar of the sea on a lonely headland, or keep them close. I cannot bring you back.

That's it, I'll call his bluff, take control.

We'll meet again. The years will dissolve. Our fingertips will be purple with blackberry juice. We'll dodge the waves. Pull razor clams. Tiptoe on the silver line. Comb the beaches for jet and singing shells, splash in rock pools.

We'll squeal as the tide comes in. Hug on the moonscape. Whistle on the path. Climb up through the faerie glen where the moss grows in soft green pillows. Shift shapes in the sea fret on the high cliff top. We'll laugh and breathe in the scent of coconut gorse.

No dark earth for us. We'll be as slippery as the seals. As light as the air, each dust particle a compressed memory. You and me. Free spirits. A boy and a girl again. We'll ride the wild white horses and shout "I love you, I love you, I love you!"

The Belle of Belfast City
by Mark McLaughlin

Longlisted, Scottish Arts Club Short Story Competition 2021

I only met Da once that I remember. A January Saturday when I was nine years old. I stared from the bottom of the hallway steps, waited for his shadow to flit across the frosted glass door panel. *Please come now, please come now.*

'I told you he wouldn't come,' said Granda.

Gran tutted and shushed him, as he muttered off towards the kitchen. I felt the softness of Gran's brown cardigan against my face, sat there, feeling too hot in anorak and scarf. The ticking of the hallway clock weighing heavy in my belly. When the doorbell eventually rang, I hurried over. Da stood tall, skinny, hair hanging at his shoulders.

'You must be Jenny.'

'Her name is Jennifer,' said Gran.

'Well … Jennifer … shall we go to the pictures?' He took my hand, his skin rough against mine. Granda reappeared, didn't shake hands the way he did when other men came to the house.

'No later than four o'clock,' he said. 'Y'hear?'

As we drove off, I wiped condensation from the car window and waved towards the house. Da's hands held the wheel and tapped along with the radio. He asked about Gran and Granda, *how about school.* So many questions, I don't know how much I answered. Soon rolling fields gave way to houses and buildings, as we neared Belfast.

I waited in the cinema foyer while he bought tickets. He walked over, head shaking.

'Sorry love,' he said. 'Wee mix up with the times. *Little Mermaid* has started, so I got *Indiana Jones* tickets. Popcorn?'

'Isn't the film starting?' I asked.

'Plenty of time,' he said.

Eventually, we made our way upstairs. Harrison Ford was already on screen, his voice boomed in the darkness. We stumbled to our seats, spilling popcorn until an usher shone her torch towards us. Whispered *sorry* as we squeezed past. I poked the straw through my Kia Ora with a twisting squeak. It tasted cool and saccharine sweet. I looked across at Da and the dust that danced in the projector beam.

When we came out it was snowing heavily. Da took me for a milkshake. He let me turn the sugar dispenser into his tea before he took a sip.

'Sure,' he said. 'That's just perfect, so it is.' He sat back smiling and sipping his tea. After a few minutes he handed me a couple of photographs from his wallet. The first was him, Mammy and me, before her accident. Me, all pink-faced in bundled blankets. The second was a photo booth strip; he made comical faces towards her, she grinned more and more until they both creased with laughter in the final shot.

'She was always laughing you know, your mammy.'

'She looks pretty.'

'Oh aye, sure was,' he said. 'None prettier.' He reached across, softly pushed my curls back from my forehead. 'You know Jenny, you look just like her, so you do.'

'Gran always says my name is Jennifer.'

'I know. We always called you Jenny. Just habit.'

When we got outside, snow had blanketed the city under the orange streetlights. My boots crunched it solid. As we walked towards the car, Da stopped by a small park.

'Jenny,' he said. 'Come with me'. He lay down in the snow, pushed his skinny legs together and apart while he moved his arms. He looked like some great bird mired in Lough Neagh mud.

'What are you doing?' I said.

'Have you never made a snow angel?'

Sure, he stood up and it looked just like Christmas. I

hurried to try and we both quickly moved around the park, laughing and making more angels. Within minutes there were a dozen.

We drove back through the city, dark but for streetlights and shop windows. At traffic lights I saw a soldier cup his hand to light a cigarette; face briefly illuminated, eyes still flitting around. The lights changed and as we moved on, Da started to sing a song Mammy used to sing to me. I joined in, quiet but growing louder as we drove along.

She is handsome. She is pretty.

She is the belle of Belfast City.

'Sure, you've a rare voice!' he said.

At home he stopped me as I opened the car door.

'You know, your Mammy would have wanted you to have these and I do too.' He handed me the strip of photographs. I stared at their faces, felt the edge of the picture through my gloves.

'Thanks,' I said. 'Will you come see me again?'

'Maybe,' he said. 'If you want me to.' As we approached the house, Gran and Granda hurried to meet us.

'Where have you been?' Gran asked. 'We were worried sick!' She hurried me in, took off my coat. 'What's this?' she said as she turned me towards Da, her hand on the back of my legs. 'Soaking wet! Soaked through to the skin!'

Granda pushed Da out the door. Gran hurried me up to the bathroom, pulled off my woollen tights.

'Some father, I tell you,' she said. Steam already rising from the bath.

'Gran,' I said. 'He's my da, so he is.'

She stopped, pulled me close.

'I know he is, Darling,' she said. 'I know he is.'

Outside Derry the rain starts. I fumble with the radio; Drive FM, DJ Tommy, *non-stop classics*. I'm on the A6 to Buncrana, Da's address in my purse, thirty years later. When Granda died, Gran gave me letters, postcards, birthday cards. All hidden away the minute they'd hit the hallway floor. After the funeral she placed them in my hand, her head shaking away my questions.

I reach Buncrana Main Street; Paddy's Day bunting still sways four days on and smokers huddle outside the Atlantic Bar. I find the address, but wait, watching the windscreen wipers slap and sluice. The rain eases and I open the door, smell saltwater. Collar high, I head over and see two girls approach the door.

'Excuse me?' I call. 'Does John McGinn live here?'

'Aye,' says the younger girl. 'But Da's no home yet.'

"Who are you?' asks the older girl.

'Jennifer,' I say. 'An old friend.'

'I'm Sarah,' says the girl. 'This is Anne.'

'Pleased to meet you both.'

'Do you want to come in?' asks Anne, 'Da won't be long.' Sarah's face is a twisted frown, her elbow sharp in Anne's side.

'Thanks,' I say. 'OK with you, Sarah?'

She nods reluctantly but opens the door. Schoolbags are dumped in the hallway. They talk quickly, arguing over TV. I scan mantlepiece photographs, wondering are these my half-sisters?

'Have you known Da long?' asks Sarah.

'I suppose I have.'

'He's never mentioned you.'

My throat dry, my fingers grip my coat.

'Well, we lost touch.'

She asks how we met and my grip tightens on my coat, but there's a key in the door and they hurry out. Voices muffled in the hallway; *do you know her, Da?* Then he's there; not as tall as I remember, hair grey and cropped.

'Hi,' he says. 'This is a surprise.'

'I was in the area …'

Anne interrupts us to show him a drawing from school.

Da's eyes shift between her, the picture and me. Smiling, nodding, until she turns back to the TV.

'I'll make tea,' he says. 'Want to help?' He turns when we're in the hallway, his voice a whisper. 'I can't do this right now.'

'I shouldn't have just turned up,' I say.

'It's just awkward. Let's take a walk.'

I stand by the door while he explains he needs to go out. Anne peers round; soft curls and freckled face. Does he sing to her? Do they make snow angels?

We go to Johnny's Café. The tea is bittersweet, dark as the Lagan. Amid the clatter of dishes, Loretta Lynn plays tinny over the radio. Da smiles.

'It's funny,' he says. 'Even if Anne hadn't said your name, I'd have recognised you.'

'Your girls seem lovely,' I say. 'You been here long?'

'A few years. It's quiet. Peaceful. And you?'

'Still in Belfast. Married with two wee boys; Kyle and James.'

'Grand,' he says. He looks away, eyes his watch. My phone weighs heavy in my pocket, all those photographs of my boys on there.

'I don't mean to cause trouble,' I say. 'When Granda died I was given your letters and I just wondered...'

'Sorry to hear about your Granda. I know he cared for you.'

I think how a mention of Da's name had Granda cursing, his newspaper rustling. I watch Da now, those years in his face.

'Looking back, me and your ma were so young when we had you and then the accident ... guess you were better off there.'

'I just wish we'd kept in touch.'

'You know, sometimes I waited at the school. Trying to see you, speak to you. I'd watch you with your pals,

206

whispering and laughing, but there was always someone picking you up.' His eyes drop towards his tea.

'Why did you stop trying?' I ask.

'I never wanted to stop. Your granda, I don't know … him high up in the RUC, me some West Belfast hippy … arse out ma jeans … he didn't want me around.'

'Did anyone think what I wanted?'

I feel his hand soft on the back of mine, but I pull back. There's a quietness between us. I stare down, pick at my nails. Think how I always picked the scabs on my knees. *You're an awful fouter.* I go the bathroom then, check my make up in the mirror. What was I thinking coming here? I should have written or called. I sit down again.

'I'm sorry,' he says.

'Sorry?'

'I don't know what else to say.'

'I was a kid, Mammy gone. I needed my father.' I'm aware then of the silence in the cafe, tutting, shaking of heads. A waitress slaps a wet, grey cloth across the tables. I look Da in the eye; same blue as me, same blue as my boys.

My phone rings, it's Gran. I put it back in my pocket, scrape my chair back and put on my coat.

'I need to go.' I say.

'Oh. Right … I'll walk you round.' He puts change on the table and we leave. We're silent. I feel I can't move quickly enough. The breeze roars muffled in my ears; a spit of rain cold on my face as I reach the car.

'Maybe I could've done more,' he says. 'But your Granda blamed me for your ma's accident. I wasn't there, but it was my old car she was driving and me she was driving to. I tried but, in the end assumed my chance had gone.'

I say nothing. He looks to hug, but I turn and open the car door. He waves and walks away. I reach for my phone but as I do, feel the envelope I'd brought him. I hesitate a few moments, then open the door and cross the road. He's on the doorstep when I get there, like he's been watching from the window.

'Here,' I say. 'I made you a copy.' He takes the strip of photo booth pictures from the envelope; he and Mammy, faces squeezing into the frame.

'Wait!' he says. He reaches into his wallet to take out the other photo he showed me all those years ago; me, him and Mammy. Faded now, colours pale as morning.

'You can have this,' he says. 'Maybe bring me a copy some time?'

'Maybe I will.'

We hug then, brief as it is before I drive away. I watch him through the rear-view mirror waving; *my da*. Soon he grows faint in the distance, just a blur of colours in the rain gathering on the rear windscreen. I turn the corner and he's gone once more. Soon, there's only the steady hum of tyres against the slick tarmac of the road.

Pyramid Scheme
by Kitty Waldron

Editor's Choice, Edinburgh Award for Flash Fiction 2021

All those hamsters. All those sleepless nights. We thought they were two males – this is how we came to have 36.

Look, I've always wanted to be on *Record Breakers*. Nobody in the world would think of *this* particular record. The pyramid has to stay standing for 30 seconds. Has to be constructed as quickly as possible. You have to use 36 hamsters, none of which must be drugged or dead. No hamsters were harmed in making my pyramids, though a few died along the way of natural causes.

Morning noon and night, my world was hamsters. So hypnotism – it came to me in a dream. I find them surprisingly suggestible. I use Roquefort and, as I swing it, their little noses follow the waft. They're all under in less than five minutes. Then they're dead easy to pile up and balance.

So here I am with Roy Castle and the McWhirters. Each hamster has been drug-tested and they're all pre-hypnotised under official adjudication.

3.2.1. Go! I start off at a good pace. And I'm breaking my own record! Just as I'm placing the 36th hamster in less than two minutes, that's when the news comes in. Someone in China has completed it in one minute 37!

I'm banging my hands and feet on the stage. And all my hamsters come round and wander off. And I'm still there on the floor as the final credits run: Oo-ooh! Dedication's what you need.

The Scottish Arts Trust Story Awards

www.storyawards.org

The Scottish Artists' Club was founded in 1873 by a group of artists and sculptors, including Sir John Steell, Sculptor to Queen Victoria, and Sir George Harvey, President of the Royal Scottish Academy. For twenty years they met in a series of premises around the West End of Edinburgh. In 1894, the building at 24 Rutland Square was purchased as a meeting place for men involved in all arts disciplines and Lay Members (those not professionally engaged in the arts) were also welcomed into the Club. To reflect the widening membership, it was renamed the Scottish Arts Club.

It was not until 1982, following contentious debate, that women were admitted as club members. In 1998, Mollie Marcellino became its first female President. Until her death in 2018, Mollie was also an avid reader for the Scottish Arts Club Short Story Competition.

The idea for the competition, which is open to writers worldwide, developed out of the Scottish Arts Club Writers Group. Alexander McCall Smith has long been a supporter and honorary member of the Club, which has sometimes featured in his Scotland Street novels. He volunteered to be our chief judge (and remained in that role until 2020 when Andrew O'Hagan took over.) Our chief judges are aided by a team of readers whose primary qualifications are a love of short fiction and a willingness to read, debate, defend and promote their favourites through successive rounds of the competition. All stories reaching the penultimate round have been read at least forty times by our readers and most have been subject to passionate debate.

The short story prize money increased from a first prize of £300 in 2014 to £1,000 by 2017. In that year we also launched the Isobel Lodge Award, named after a dear friend and member of the Writers Group. This prize, which rose to £750 in 2020 is given to the top story entered in the competition by an unpublished writer born, living or studying in Scotland.

In 2018 we introduced the Edinburgh Award for Flash Fiction, with novelist Sandra Ireland as the chief judge. Sandra won the first of our short story competitions with her story, *The Desperation Game*, which lends its title to this anthology. In 2021, celebrated authors Zoë Strachan and Louise Welsh took over as the flash fiction judges. In 2023, the flash fiction prize rises to £1,000 and the Golden Hare Award for the top flash fiction entry from Scotland rises to £500.

We enjoy celebrating the work of our short story finalists at the annual and always sold-out Story Awards Dinner held at the Scottish Arts Club – and the flash fiction writers at the highly entertaining Flash Bash.

The story awards are managed through the Scottish Arts Trust, (registered charity number SC044753). All funds raised through our competitions, which also include the annual Scottish Portrait Awards, are used to promote the arts in Scotland. Learn more about the Trust at www.scottishartstrust.org

To apply for our awards – go to www.storyawards.org

- Enter the Scottish Arts Club Short Story Competition from 1 December to 28/29 February – open to writers over 16 years worldwide and stories on any topic up to 2,000 words.

- Apply for the Isobel Lodge Award by entering the short story competition and indicating on the entry form that you are an unpublished writer resident in Scotland.

- Enter the Edinburgh Award for Flash Fiction from 1 June to 31 August – open to writers over 16 years worldwide and stories on any topic up to 250 words.

- Apply for the Golden Hare Award by entering the flash fiction competition and indicating on the entry form that you are resident in Scotland.

We look forward to reading your stories!

Sara Cameron McBean,
Director, Scottish Arts Trust Story Awards

Acknowledgements

Our special thanks to Andrew O'Hagan who continued as the chief judge of the short story award in 2021 and to award-winning authors Zoë Strachan and Louise Welsh who took over as chief judges of the flash fiction award. Louise and Zoë provided brilliant insights during the Flash Bash which was forced on-line due to Covid 19.

We are very grateful to John Lodge whose donations support the Isobel Lodge Award, which brings such encouragement to countless unpublished short story writers in Scotland. Thanks also to Mark Jones whose donations support the Golden Hare Award that has helped to promote interest in the flash format across Scotland.

Our teams of dedicated readers reviewed and discussed over 1,500 entries to the short and flash fiction competitions in 2021. We are in awe of the time, energy and commitment the readers bring to successive rounds of these competitions and their passion as they make the case for the stories they love to progress through the competition – several of the stories in this volume were wild-carded into the anthology by passionate readers who refused to let these gems slip away.

We are indebted to Dai Lowe who works tirelessly as our story awards administrator, to Siobhán Coward who manages the short story readers and to Linda Grieg who does the same for the flash fiction teams. Our thanks also to Gordon Mitchell whose wonderful paintings give our anthologies and the Scottish Arts Trust Story Awards website such a distinctive visual style.

Finally, a huge thank you to all the writers who have imagined, drafted, written, re-written and submitted stories in 2021. Your stories are packed with inspiration and creative passion. We look forward to reading more!

Published by the Scottish Arts Trust
www.scottishartstrust.org
Registered Charity SC044753
All funds raised are used to support the arts in Scotland